Diary of the Underworld

Look for More Terrorlands Books
by Marco Chu Kwan Ching

TERRORLAND

DIARY OF THE UNDERWORLD

MARCO CHU KWAN CHING

A
PEAR
PAPERBACK

ISBN: 978-0-6482760-6-7

First printing in 2017
Second printing in 2019

PART 1

1

I remembered it was June last year; I began to suffer from insomnia for the first time in my life.

And believe me, it certainly wasn't a wonderful experience.

The problem was mild at the beginning.

Then my sleeping disorder just got worse and worse...

It reached a point where my sleep cycle was devastated.

"Alice, time to see Dr. Amy," Mom shouted from downstairs.

"Just a second," I yelled.

Doctor Amy is my personal doctor to treat my insomnia symptom. She is good. I don't mean the sleeping pills she prescribed, but her Zimbabwean. It just works remarkably well to put me to sleep.

The first time I read Dr. Amy's name card, I could hardly pronounce her surname name right.

I guess super-tag is the closest pronunciation to *Supratik*, right?

Anyway, I have been seeing Dr. Amy for almost two weeks now.

So far, most of her therapies were cosmetic to me.

And today, we are going to try a different therapy – hypnotherapy.

Please don't ask me the details about hypnotherapy. All I know is it uses the most powerful part of the subconscious mind to change behavior and feelings.

Hopefully, it will work on me.

"Alice, you have an appointment at 10:30 am. I need at least half an hour to get there," my mom began to stress.

"I am coming, Mom," I replied as I took my time to put on my make-up.

Oops. I have forgotten to introduce myself. My name is Alice. And I am thirteen. I have big, beautiful eyes, an adorable pointed nose, and curly brown hair.

Above all, I love my lips most.

I loved wearing lipsticks.

I think a signature lipstick gives you an identity.

Every girl in the world can swipe on a red lipstick and look amazing, but as much as I love red, I am not going for such a bold look.

Hummm…

What color should I choose today?

Crimson? Purple? Pink?

What do you think?

I was scrambling inside my makeup case, searching for the color of my day.

I just love makeup so much. I can spend hours and hours in my room trying to get that perfect look.

"I am waiting…" Mom called again.

I peered down at Mom from upstairs. She was gazing at her watch every two seconds.

I could tell Mom was stressed out already.

She was muttering to herself at the door entrance.

I have a bad feeling I will get in trouble soon.

Well, I better hurry.

I gave myself one last look in the mirror, tidied up my hair, and hopped downstairs to meet Mom.

"Good morning," I greeted Mom.

"We will be late," Mom sounded impatient.

"What is the matter? I am going there to take a nap anyway," I said as I put on my heels.

"Alice, it is not taking a nap. It is hypnosis. We want to find out what is wrong with you. By the way, no high heels today. You need to wear comfortable clothing and shoes. We are seeing Dr. Amy," Mom demanded.

"Fine." I obeyed as I swapped it with a sneaker instead.

Mom can be quite strict sometimes. We even have a family rule of conduct fridge magnet stuck to our refrigerator door.

As usual, schoolwork always comes before TV.

But, overall, Mom is excellent.

She has been relaxed on me since I had this weird insomnia symptom.

The trip to Dr. Amy's office was exhausting.

A trip that was supposed to take no more than half an hour ended up taking us an hour instead.

Well, I can't blame anyone. Today is Saturday. And Saturday means shopping day.

Kensington Medical Center towered above us like a white mansion as we drove past its entrance. The Medical Center was cylindrical in design, surrounded a large public garden with a pond. In front of the medical center was an oval roundabout. Four pillars were supporting shade fins in the front entrance to provide shelters.

"Rabbits!" I cried in excitement when I spotted two rabbits chasing each other in the garden.

We entered the medical center through an automatic glass door, and the smell of disinfectant invaded my nostrils.

A long queue of patients was lining up in front of the reception desk.

An angry man with a wrist band was complaining about the wait.

A doctor schooled a child for cycling in the corridor.

Sitting on the bench was a woman short of breath and gasping. It seemed like she was suffering from asthma.

Mom told me to put on a mask because of the germs in the hospital.

Then she checked the directory near the entrance.

Apparently, Dr. Amy is located on the second level of the medical center.

Dr. Amy's clinic used to be located in Richville – a suburb not far from us. But the increase in rent and the lack of people forced her to relocate. It was only last week that she informed us her new office is in a commercial space in Kensington Medical Center.

Honestly, I prefer Richville to Kensington Medical Center.

This hospital is too crowded and noisy.

As Mom and I walked towards the elevator, a kid was whining to his parents.

"Mom, I don't want to see the doctor. I want an apple instead," the boy cried.

"Why do you want an apple now?" His parents frowned.

"An apple a day keeps the doctor away."

Funny kids. I wish I had a little brother like this, so my mom would focus less on me.

Well, maybe I should request it tonight. It is never too late to have a brother, right?

Ding!

The elevator door finally slid open, and a middle age woman with a cleaning cart moved out of the elevator.

"Excuse me! Excuse me!" The middle age woman demanded everyone to back away. Her mop and broom were upside down. Chlorine was tilting left and right inside the yellow bucket.

Drops of chemicals spilled on the floor as the middle age woman displaced.

Then, a swarm of people rushed into the elevator, and we couldn't fit in.

Mom rolled her eyes, and I gave her a helpless look.

"Maybe we will wait for the next one," I suggested.

"Maybe we should go by the stairs instead," Mom gave me a sharp glance.

The second level was a long, spacious hallway with polished linoleum flooring. The wall was creamy. The air had an odor of bleach. Everything was brightly lid.

It didn't take us long before we found Dr. Amy's office.

"Hello," Dr. Amy greeted us with her musical Zimbabwean accent as we entered her room.

"Hello, Dr. Amy, your new place is wonderful!" I smiled.

I must admit Dr. Amy spent quite a lot of effort in decorating this room.

I could see the four corners of her office were wrapped with a wallpaper of a lake in paranormal view. The reflection of the lake was so realistic that I had a feeling I was no longer in a hospital.

The background music inside the room featured the sound of running water.

Even before the therapy, I could already feel the unique, relaxing energy sweep over my body.

"Wow, it is a great place," I exclaimed.

Mom apologized to Dr. Amy for being late and left me with Dr. Amy for the therapy.

"How do you feel?" Dr. Amy asked as she rested me on the hypnotherapist's chair.

"Well. I still have difficulty falling asleep during the night. I feel tired during the day," I replied.

"I suppose the medication did not work too well on you," Dr. Amy concluded.

"Do you know what is really happening to me?" I asked.

"People have insomnia for many reasons. It may be because of tension. It may be they have unhealthy lifestyles and poor sleeping habits. It may be because of love problems. Do you have a boyfriend?" Dr. Amy asked.

"No way," I giggled.

"You are a pretty girl," Dr. Amy appraised.

"Thank you."

Dr. Amy helped me to adjust the hypnosis chair and asked me to sit back and relax.

"Hypnotherapy is a beautiful tool that enables anyone to have focused attention in a truly relaxed state to assist in finding their own true answers," Dr. Amy said as she swung a pendulum in front of me. "Now, look at it and tell me what you see."

My eyes followed …

Left and right… left and right…

The pendulum took a tiny movement at the beginning and magnified.

Left and right… left and right…

Everything began to turn blurred.

And I began to speak.

2

I was standing at the mouth of a cave alone.

Alone.

Behind me was a wide ledge.

I peered down and saw ocean waves crashing against the lowest rocks, spraying surf in every direction.

Above my head, I could see a full moon drifting and disappear behind the heavy clouds.

Then, I felt large raindrops on my head, then my face.

The gust of howling winds was swirling heavy rain around me.

The rain pattered against the rock, creating sounds like drumbeats.

I was trembling.

I felt so cold and lost.

Where am I? Why am I here?

I tried to search for my mobile phone to call for help, but I couldn't find it.

This is no good...

Rain got heavier by the second, and I was soaking wet.

My body was shivering in the cold.

A jagged bolt of lightning stretched across the sky, and the mouth of the cave was revealed.

It seemed that I had no choice but to enter the cave.

I peered into the cave opening.

How deep was the cave?

"Hello," I yelled. "Anybody here?"

My voice echoed in the hollow cave.

Then I saw a glimmering light flickering from inside, as if calling to me.

My sneaker made a loud squish sound as I slid on the wet, damp cave floor.

It is slippery. I realized.

The rocks must have been damp from the storm.

I continued to follow the light.

The cave was like a labyrinth.

I lost count of how many twists and turns I made.

I kept following the light. It seemed like they processed some irresistible magical power and attracted me like a magnet.

I could hear the constant dripping sound of water.

So loud. So clear.

I made a turn into another narrow, curving tunnel.

Suddenly, I heard something…

It sounded like something was fluttering rapidly. The sound was soft at first, then louder, closer.

Then a sour odor swept over me.

Yuck.

"What is it?" My voice came out trembling.

Before I could find out what was happening, the dark cave ceiling crumbled on me.

I screamed at the top of my lungs and tried to run away.

But, I slip and landed onto the wet stone floor.

Whoosh!

I felt something brush over my neck. And something zoomed right past by shoulder.

"Get away from me! Get away from me!" I covered my head with my hands.

Slowly, I began to see the shadowy forms of the creatures shooting past.

Back and forth. Back and forth.

I raised my eyes and saw their eyes lock on mine.

I saw bats. Huge bats. Thousands of bats with bloodshot eyes, flapping and fluttering, whistling and hissing.

I must have awakened them when I entered their chamber.

And they all seemed hungry...

My eyes darted left and right. I was slowly crawling backwards with my trembling hands.

Just as the creature dove towards me for another attack, a musical voice from nowhere stopped them and put the creatures back into hibernation.

"Wh-who is that," my voice came out dry.

I sat on the damp cave floor, still like a statue, too frightened to move.

"Don't be afraid," a ghostly voice from nowhere whispered. Dry as death.

"Show yourself," I tried to scream, but it came out in a choke.

"Come, young one," the musical voice hypnotized me.

Slowly, I got up and followed the sound unconsciously.

I made a turn at the far end of the tunnel, and it suddenly widened into a deep, round chamber.

In the middle of the chamber was a decayed rock in a dish shape.

"Hello," I whispered and wrapped myself with my arm as I walked inside.

My voice echoed off the wall and the high ceiling.

A rat scampered from behind the decayed rock in the middle, and my heart almost skipped a beat.

Disgusting.

I swear to God I hate rats. They are the most horrible creatures God ever created. They are a plague to people. They steal cheese. They carry disease and fleas.

Do you know rats were the carriers of Black Death and caused the death of 75 to 200 million people in Europe during the 12th century?

Just before I decided to give this chamber a miss, something from the dish-like rock caught the corner of my eyes.

Is there something over there?

I took a step forward. And another step.

Then, I saw it.

It was a vintage book.

3

My dream ended abruptly when an alarm rang.

Once again, I was shaken back into reality.

I laid on the hypnotherapist's chair, debating whether to get up.

My muscles were weak.

Everything was blurry and brightly lit.

I blinked a few times and saw Dr. Amy's face.

"How do you feel?" Dr. Amy asked gently.

"Dr. Amy," I cried in fright.

I lost count of how many times I have had this dream.

The cave. The bat. The voice.

Everything seemed so real.

"It's okay," Dr. Amy wrapped her arms around me and patted my back.

Before I realized it, I was sweating all over.

"Dr. Amy, is it normal for me to have the same dream over and over again?" I asked nervously.

"Child, don't be afraid. Usually, emotions or things happen in our life to trigger our dreams. If you repeatedly have the same dream, that means your subconscious is trying to send you a message." Dr. Amy explained.

"But the one that I am having is different. It...it is scary...I can still remember the dream. It ...it is a nightmare..." I choked with panic.

Dr. Amy walked towards her desk to grab a folder and poured me a cup of water.

"Alice. You are not alone. I have had patients who have recurring dreams like you. One of the patients dreamt being chased by a woolly mammoth when he was somewhere in an African desert." Dr. Amy referenced her files in the folder.

"Chased by a woolly mammoth? I wonder what that feels like." I laughed.

"Do you know what that dream means?" Dr. Amy asked.

"Is it because that patient had bad experience with elephants?" I guessed.

"Well, it can be. But, the dream also tells me the patient is trying to get away from something in life. He is running from or trying to hide from something he needs to face. It can also be a feeling he wants to avoid, a conflict he doesn't want to handle, or a memory he would rather forget," Dr. Amy explained.

I nodded in agreement.

What Dr. Amy was saying is so true.

"I also had a recurring dream at one stage in my life," Dr. Amy revealed.

This is the first time I have found something in common with the doctor.

"Do you have a recurring dream? What is it? Please tell

me," I exclaimed.

"I did. I remembered I often had a recurring dream while I was seven or eight. In the dream, I recalled myself standing on the edge of my blue leather sofa at home, while gazing at the sky through my floor to ceiling balcony window. I kept looking at the sky. So focused. I sensed myself floating through the window slowly. Then up and up I flew. When I looked down, everything was getting smaller and smaller. My home. The people on the street were like ants." Dr. Amy smiled.

"How do you interpret this dream?" I continued to ask.

"Well, it is kind of hard to say. I lived with my grandparents, and I moved back to live with my parents at the age of eight. I guess I had more school work ever since. So, that is why I have this kind of weird recurring dream. I read that dreams about flying is an expression of freedom," Dr. Amy replied.

"Do you still have this dream now?" I questioned.

"No. I never have this dream anymore, since I discovered Lucid dreaming," Dr. Amy shared her experience.

"Lucid dreaming?" I gave her a curious gaze.

"It is like you are aware when you are dreaming," Dr. Amy said as she wrote something on her notes.

"How can I have Lucid dreams, too?" I wondered.

"Here it is. Take this. Go see Father William McNeil. I think he might be a better person to help you."

4

Shortly after my hypnotherapy session, Mom arrived.

Dr. Amy had a private conversation with her about my situation.

I was waiting for them in the guest room.

When Mom finally came out, I saw her worried expression.

"Mom, what is wrong?" I asked.

"It's nothing. You won't be seeing Dr. Amy anymore," Mom started.

"But I will be seeing Father William McNeil, right?" I forced a smile, trying to be optimistic.

"Do you know who Father William McNeil is?" Mom asked.

"Well, I guess he is a priest. I don't know." I shrugged.

"Yes. A priest. You are suffering from insomnia, and Dr. Amy asked you to seek help from a priest." Mom rolled her eyes.

I know exactly how Mom feels. She feels insulted by Dr. Amy's recommendation.

"By the way, you won't be seeing Dr. Amy anymore. She

said she can't help you," Mom added.

Why does Mom always have to make things sound worse than it seemed?

We left the hospital shortly after.

Mom was planning to drive me home, but was interrupted by a phone call from Aunty Betty. The truth is that Mom had almost forgotten she has a gathering she must attend in the afternoon, so she could only drop me off at the park nearest our home instead.

That wasn't too bad.

I wanted to be alone and have some fresh air in the park, anyway.

When Mom left, I started to relax.

It is such a beautiful afternoon.

I don't want to waste it spending the rest of the day at home.

Bright sunlight made the tall grass sparkle all around me.

I shielded my eyes with my hands to search around. The narrow road curved through a forest of Jacaranda as far as I could see.

It is absolutely sensational.

I love everything purple.

I followed a short path to a low, sloping hill.

Two cute squirrels scurried past playfully in front my feet.

"Hello, little squirrels, how are you today?" I cried happily.

The two squirrels blinked at me for a second and then wrinkled their noses to greet me. Then they wobbled rapidly over the grass as they competed for the acorn.

I danced along, singing, making up funny words to songs I knew.

Look at love
How it tangles
With the one fall in love

Look at spirit
How it fuses with earth
Giving it new life

By the time I reached the top of the hill, I saw an ocean of purple flowers blanketing the park.

Even from a distance, the scent of lavender invaded my nostrils.

I stretched myself, overlooking the beautiful scene below.

"Beautiful," I heard a guy's voice interrupt me from behind.

When I looked back I was stunned. I saw a guy, who looked a few years older than me. He wore a black silk shirt with leather cuffs. He had rich chocolate curly hair. His eyes were mesmerizing deep ocean blue. He had distinct cheekbones and an angular jaw. Somehow, his pale skin made him look devilishly handsome.

"The flowers, my lady" the guy smiled, a hard line drawn across his face.

My lady? He is kind of cute.

"Where are you from?" I smiled back.

"A long way from here," he replied.

Somehow, I sensed some sorrow behind that smile.

I felt embarrassed. Although many guys approached me in school, my heart never beat like this quick before.

What is happening to me?

I am not afraid, but I am not relaxed enough to make a genuine smile either.

I need to leave. But, then, I want to stay…

Finally, I dropped my gaze.

"Welcome back," I tried to evade his glance and began to walk away.

"Why think separately of this life and the next, when one is born from the last…" the guy sang.

Huh? How did he know I like this poem?

I was held captive by his words.

"It is my favorite poem. How do you know it?" I turned around and studied him.

"Time is always too short for those who need it, but for those who love, it lasts forever." The guy slowly walked toward me.

My heart was pounding fast.

My purple eyes locked on his.

"I… I am Alice." I introduced myself.

"Vlad." The guy introduced his name.

He held my hand gently and kissed it.

Before I could react, he took out a purple rose magically from behind him.

It is my favorite purple rose!

My face turned red.

"Why a purple rose?" I pretended I don't like it.

"Purple rose is a symbol of enchantment. They are long-lasting." Vlad flashed me a smile.

We sat together silently on a slope.

Vlad told me he is from Romania in Southeastern Europe. He said Romania is a beautiful place, and the name Romania comes from the Latin word Romanus, which means citizens of the Roman Empire.

"So, are you a descendent of Julius Caesar?" I joked.

"Maybe I am. Maybe I am not. But, do you know why such a powerful empire falls?" Vlad asked.

"Is it because the Roman Empire lost great leaders like Julius Caesar?" I guessed.

"The Fall of Roman legion happened for many reasons. One main reason is inflation," Vlad replied.

"Inflation?" I was eager to know more.

"Back then, the Romans were using *Denarius* as money. It was a silver coin with 90% silver. But, since there was a limit supply of silver entering the empire, Roman spending was limited by the amount of *Denarius* that could be minted. They did not have enough money to support their war. One day, the Romans found a way to work around this. They decreased the purity of their coinage, so they were able to make more *Denarius*. But, more money in circulation diluted the value of *Denarius*. In the end, *Denarius* became worthless. The economy of Rome was paralyzed," Vlad explained.

Vlad seemed to be quite intelligent for his age.

Our eyes made contact. I felt an explosion within me. The feeling was so strange. It stretched through my whole body.

It seemed that I knew Vlad for a very long time…

"Sorry if I bored you," Vlad apologized.

"I love hearing your stories," I stammered.

"But, Romania is a place of rich history. It has many

beautiful castles. If you have a chance to come to Romania, I will give you a tour." Vlad stood up and stretched.

A gust of wind made a column of lavender flowers swirl up in front of us.

Everything felt so silent, so peaceful, so relaxing.

"Do you know life's most beautiful things are not seen with the eyes, but felt with the heart?" Vlad said.

"I do." I brushed my hair out of my face and gently replied.

I lost track of how long I had stayed in the park.

It was twilight already.

The sky had darkened.

Vlad and I enjoyed the stunning purple sunset above the lavender field.

Everything looked like an oil painting.

"Vlad, I am afraid I have to go home. Thanks for everything today," I said reluctantly and began to walk away.

"Are you leaving already?" Vlad asked.

"Yes. My parents will worry if I don't go back," I replied honestly. "Don't worry. we can catch up. I just live a few blocks away."

"Very well. It was nice to meet you," Vlad replied in a sad smile.

"Alice, where have you been?" Mom asked as soon as I entered the house.

Dad gave me a throat slash sign and hinted I am in trouble.

But, his white chef hat on his head made him looked funny. It eased the tension.

"Mom, I just went out for a walk," I said as I took off my sneakers.

"It is six o' clock now. I remembered I dropped you at one o' clock in the park a few blocks away," Mom scolded.

"Mom, it is okay. Alice is a big girl now. Maybe it is time to give her a bit more freedom." Dad brushed his hands against Mom's shoulder and gave me a wink.

"You are not helping her. You are spoiling her," Mom argued.

"Sorry, Mom, I won't do that next time," I apologized.

My stomach growled, and I tried to silence the rumbling.

Then I smelled something good.

"You are hungry. Go take a bath. Dinner is almost

ready," Dad ordered.

"What are you cooking, Dad?" I asked and peeped inside the kitchen.

Then I saw a can of beer stuck under the chicken's butt. It is Dad's traditional way to make the chicken taste sweeter.

"Balsamic marinated steak and chicken on the grill. Your favorite." Dad grinned.

"I love you, Dad!" I gave him a big hug.

"I smelled lavender," Dad exclaimed. "Have you been to the garden?"

"Yes. I have! You have got to see it. I saw an ocean of lavender blanketing the garden!" I exclaimed.

"Interesting. It is only January. I thought the lavender blossom would be somewhere starting from April," Dad raised his eyebrows.

"Oh well, maybe it had an early start this year." I shrugged.

I spent the rest of the night watching Titanic with Mom and Dad. Mom seemed to enjoy every bit of the movie, while Dad was snoring all the way.

I felt there is a lot of truth when the movie says a woman's heart is a deep ocean of secrets.

My mind was filled with the moments I had with Vlad.

But, will I see him again?

When it was about eleven, everyone started to go to bed.

"Try to sleep, all right?" Mom patted me on the shoulder.

"Goodnight, Mom and Dad." I gave my parents a hug. I had one last shower, removed my makeup, and brushed my teeth before going to bed.

I pulled on my pajamas and looked at myself in the sliding mirrored door of the build in wardrobes.

I looked exhausted. My face looked pale as a ghost.

"Alice, you have got to sleep tonight," I promised myself.

Then, something on my desk caught the corner of my eyes.

It was the purple rose Vlad gave me.

I opened the window in my room to let in some fresh air, and a soft breeze invaded the room.

It was a clear, cloudless night. Thousands of stars twinkled in the sky.

I gazed down at the empty street.

It was illuminated by the artificial yellow glow of the streetlamps.

Vlad. I wondered what is he doing now.

I uttered a deep sigh and switched off the light.

Then I was alone in darkness, once again.

I stared at the blank ceiling.

People used to tell me counting sheep would put people to sleep, but I don't know why it doesn't work on me.

By the time I counted to two thousand, I was still wide-awake.

The night wore on, and crazy thoughts tumbled in my mind.

I remembered I read an old story about Rip Van winkle by Washington Irving. The main character went to sleep after taking an elixir of wine. By the time he woke up, everything was different. His dog was gone. He recognized no one in his town.

I wondered if it was only a fairy tale.

What if it happens to me?

I tossed and turned in the bed, but couldn't find a comfortable position.

Soon, the bed became a tangle of quilt covers.

Insomnia haunts my nights; fatigue rules my days.

I don't want it to be another long night.

My throat was dry.

Maybe I should have a cup of milk and then come back to sleep.

I have to sleep at all cost, I decided.

I got out of bed. It was already one o' clock in the morning.

The floor was freezing cold.

I tried to turn the doorknob of my room as quietly as possible. After all, I don't want to wake up Mom and Dad.

By the time I got out of my room, I could hear Dad's snoring thundering through the house like a raging storm.

I pointed my toes down as I walked down the stairs, but they quaked a few times under my feet.

By the time I was downstairs, I fumbled in the dark for the light switch.

I stumbled into the kitchen and stood next to the refrigerator.

Great. Let's see what is inside.

Just as I was about to open the door, something from the window caught the corner of my eyes.

I spun around and saw a shadow outside the window.

Who is that? Who would sneak around outside my house at this time of the night? Is…is it a thief? Should I wake up Mom and Dad?

Questions rotated like a carousel around my head.

"Don't be afraid," a familiar voice whispered in my head.

Slowly, my mind became cloudy. I couldn't think clearly.

I tried to shake the voice away, but it won over my curiosity.

"Who is that? I … I remember your voice," I demanded.

Then the shadow swiftly moved away from my view. And my mind was a flashback of scattered images of my dream.

The cave. The voice. The book.

Everything seemed so real.

My instincts tell me to that whoever is hiding outside my window must be related to my dream.

I quickly grabbed my coat and key from the sofa and hurried outside the house.

The streetlamps threw a pool of dim yellow onto the cobbled pavement.

Crickets were chirping in the silence of the night.

A mysterious man in a top hat and long black coat turned and disappeared at the corner of the street.

Is he the one who hid outside my window?

When I spun around, I saw no one else on the street.

I followed the man slowly, and then increased my pace.

The streets that were familiar to me in the morning looked foreign at night.

The thin mist and fog at night danced across the street and made everything hazy.

I lost count of how many corners I turned.

All of a sudden, I felt like a character lost in some dark fantasy.

Just when I turned another corner, I arrived at a wide avenue.

A river of cars was parked parallel to the curb on my left.

On my right, security gates over retails shops lined the street.

Trees were lined up like security guards.

An ambulance drove by on the opposite side of the road at a breathtaking speed. Its flashing yellow and blue streak blinded me temporarily before passing and disappearing.

I felt eerie walking along in the middle of the night.

But, something inside me made me unable to resist.

Where did the man go?

I checked at the dark pavement ahead but saw no signs of him.

How could I possibly lose him?

Just as I was about to give up, I spotted an old woman in a hood sitting cross-legged beside the corner of a convenience store.

The woman encircled herself with candles while muttering to herself.

Perhaps, she might have seen where the mysterious man in the top hat had gone.

Step by step, I walked towards the old woman.

Even from a distance, I could see wrinkles on every surface of her exposed skin. Her hair was grey and dirty. Little creatures were crawling in and out of her hair. Worst of all, she smelled like she just came out of the sewage.

By the time the old woman saw me, she raised her head and grinned at me with her yellow and black teeth.

I swallowed hard.

I felt my guts twist when I exchanged a glance with this ugly woman.

The snake-like glare from her eyes gave me goose-bumps.

Is she a beggar? What is she doing with the candles in the middle of the night?

"You looked troubled, young lady," the old woman motioned me to come over with her long fingernails.

"Ho-how do you know?" I took a step forward but kept a safe distance.

"I have read too many people in my lifetime," the old

woman replied. "You seemed troubled by a dream."

A dream? How did she know I am troubled by a dream?

"Who are you?" I asked cautiously.

"It is not important who I am," the old woman spoke.

"Why are you lighting up candles on the street?" I asked.

"Young lady, these candles are for me to see things. To see what others cannot see," the old woman hissed. Her eyes glittered.

What does she mean by seeing other things people cannot see?

"Can you tell what is wrong with me? I have this strange insomnia symptom that disturbs my sleep. Sometimes, when I take a nap, I have this strange recurring dream. I saw myself in a cave. I heard strange voices, bats, and a book. Every time I go to sleep, the dream reveals itself more and more," I explained.

The old woman studied me for a long time.

Then her eyes opened wide. Her expression changed. Her face twisted as if she was psychotic.

"Is there something wrong?" I was confused.

"I am sorry I cannot help you." Her voice trembled.

The arc of golden candlelight flickered and grew dimmer as the wax melted.

"*Denizen of chaos and Erebus, and of the unfathomable abyss! Haunter of the deep…*" the old woman chanted. Her body was shivering.

"Hey, are you okay?" I was scared.

"Th…that vision you have was not a dream. It…it is a curse…" the old woman murmured.

She waved her hands and tried to drive me away.

"What curse? Do you know something? Can you help me?" I cried.

"That accursed book…" The old woman shook her head vigorously.

Then, I saw thousands of spiders were crawling out from her hair.

"Nooooooo, it is happening again," the old woman cried in fear.

Then, an orange hued ray appeared behind the buildings. Endless rays of pink shimmered between the gaps of the leaves.

By the time I turned back, the old woman and the candles disappeared into thin air.

"Alice!" I heard familiar voices calling from a distance.

When I turned around to find out who it was, I was shocked by who I saw.

7

"Alice! What is going on with you? Why are you out-side at night?" Mom gasped, her eyes wide open in fright.

Dad was catching up with her from behind in pajamas.

"Wh- Who are you talking to?" Dad added.

I swear to God I had never seen Mom and Dad so wor-ried in my entire life.

"I...I..." I stammered.

I tried to explain, but my mind went blank.

There is no way I could explain this – not in a way my parents would understand.

"Are you sleep-walking?" Dad studied me seriously.

Dad, that is a good one.

"Sleepwalking?" Mom frowned.

"Yes. Sleepwalking," Dad repeated and continued to explain his hypothesis. "Sleepwalking can be simply sitting up in bed and looking around, to walking around the room or house, leaving the house, and even travelling a long distance. In fact, it can be quite dangerous not to wake a sleepwalker. Alice is sleep deprived. I think that is what makes her sleepwalk at night."

"Dad, Alice's insomnia problem is getting worse and worse. We tried medication and hypnosis but nothing seemed to work." Mom started to sob.

"Honey, it is okay. We will face this together." Dad hugged Mom.

I felt guilty.

Did I sleep walk? Was everything an illusion just then?

It seemed that my insomnia has been haunting not only me, but my entire family.

"Mom, Dad, I am all right. I am sorry…" I whispered.

"It is okay sweetheart; everything will be okay," Mom gave me a big hug.

"Now, everyone back home to sleep. Later, we will have a brunch. Everyone must be tired. We have been out the whole night." Dad yawned.

The sky continued to brighten on our way home.

Darkness had surrendered to the light.

I still have a lot of questions in my mind. But, I guess they were unimportant as of now.

I gave the avenue one last look.

Everything was a silhouette against a crimson sky.

Dad told me he had sleep paralysis when he was my age.

What is sleep paralysis?

Well, it is sort of like a state between wakefulness and sleep. During sleep paralysis, you will be unable to move, speak, or react to whatever is happening.

Dad said he had strange visions and heard a demonic voice when he was trying to resist. He said there was a time he witnessed a shadowy humanoid figure lurking outside his bedroom window. Then, another time, he felt suffocated, as if something was exerting pressure on his chest, making him feel difficult to breath.

"Your Grandma worried so much that she brought me to visit different doctors," Dad continued his story.

"Did the doctors manage to help?" I asked curiously.

"No. Nothing worked on me." Dad shook his head.

Mom placed some baked eggs in ham baskets on our plate as she walked out from the kitchen.

It was mouthwatering.

"Morning, what are the two of you talking about?"

Mom asked as she joined us at the table.

"Oh, I am just sharing my sleep paralysis experiences with Alice, so that she won't feel unnatural," Dad said.

"So how did you get rid of sleep paralysis?" I continued to ask.

"Ever since I met your mother, my sleep paralysis just disappeared like it never happened," Dad joked.

"How sweet of you," Mom said as she spoon-fed Dad the baked eggs.

Dad looked delighted.

"Really?" I raised my eyebrows.

"Alice, sometimes you need to focus on other things in life," Dad advised. "Look at this baked eggs in ham baskets; if you don't try it, how do you know it will live up to its name?"

Perhaps, Dad is right. Maybe if I focus on other things in life, I will eventually get better.

"So, what do we have for today?" Dad asked. He took a quick sip of the cappuccino, sat back, and relaxed.

"It is Sunday. Maybe we can go to church," Mom suggested.

"Brilliant idea." Dad quickly agreed as if he planned this conversation with Mom beforehand.

After we had our brunch, Dad went to do the dishes. Mom and I went back to our room to dress up.

As usual, I took ages to get ready.

When I was finally done, Mom and Dad were already waiting inside the car.

Mom and Dad are Christians. So am I. They brought me to baptism when I was a baby girl. Dad told me how the priest sprinkled water on my forehead. After this holy sacrament, I have been baptized.

However, we have not been to church in two years.

So, I guess we might a bit foreign to other Christians in the church today.

One of the lessons I remembered from church is the evil of negations. Words like "don't, not, and won't" steal our freedom given by God. The priest in charge challenged us to use only positive phrasing. He said language is a very powerful tool that instructs both our conscious and subconscious mind. That is why we have to use it carefully.

After a while, we arrived at a magnificent building made of old stones and stained glass windows. Even from a distance, I could hear the organ music and smell the fresh flowers. Children were chasing each other at the entrance, and their parents were trying to stop them.

There we were, standing in front of St Mary Cathedral.

When we stepped inside the church, a wave of love and harmony swept over me.

"It is mass time," Mom whispered as we sneaked inside to grab our spots on an empty bench.

I saw some children in the choir giggling with one another though the service. The little ones were playing with their smocks. Their parents flickered their eyes to scowl at them from below the stage.

But, when they sang, all was forgiven. Their voices were angelic and embraced the whole cathedral and up the pillars.

I felt peace of mind too. Maybe we should come to the church more often.

When the mass was finished, the children obediently

followed one another down the stage.

"How did you sing so well," a parent in front of us asked her children.

"It is because of Father William McNeil's chocolate cake." The children smiled.

Did the children just say Father William McNeil?

Then I looked at my parents.

"Is that Alice?" An old man in clerical clothing approached me.

"This is Father William," Mom introduced the priest to me.

"He-hello Father William. I have heard about you," I stammered.

"Of course you have, Alice. Father William was the priest who christened you when you were a baby girl," Dad exclaimed.

"It has been a long time. Alice, I have heard much about you too. Congratulations on getting into a selective Christian high school," Father William cheered me up.

"Well, I suppose Mom and I will let you spend some time to catch up with Father William." Dad tapped on my shoulder.

Soon, the cathedral was emptied.

I waved good-bye with my parents and followed Father William to the inner part of the cathedral.

Church staff and volunteers greeted the priest as we walked past them.

I walked by a room and saw groups of young people having bible study together.

We followed the corridor, turned left, and arrived inside Father William's office.

I must admit Father William has good taste in furnishing. His room was a classic Victorian style library with a high ceiling. A large carpet was placed on top of the hardwood flooring. Rows of antique oak bookshelves paneled the walls. Above the bookshelves were paintings on renaissance and angels. It is just remarkable.

Father William settled me on his expensive leather sofa and handed me a cup of water.

"Alice, I heard that you have trouble sleeping," Father William began to ask.

"Yes. It all started June last year, since I had this insomnia. It has been haunting me ever since," I replied.

"Did you see anything unnatural?" Father William asked.

"Well. I …" I tried to explain but didn't know where to begin.

"Take it slowly and tell me everything," Father William encouraged.

"I had this strange dream when I closed my eyes for a nap in the morning. I saw myself standing on the mouth of a cliff in a stormy night. Below me was a wide ledge. Then I walked inside that cave. It was damp and dark. I saw bats… and I heard a ghostly voice that led me to a chamber. It looked like a catacomb. In the middle of the chamber was a …" I spoke with my eyes closed. I tried to recall everything I saw in that dream.

"What is it?" Father William pursued.

"It was a vintage book," I finally said.

Father William's expression slowly turned serious.

"Father William, do you know something?" I asked suspiciously.

Father William studied me and then decided to speak.

"In fact, you are not the only one who is troubled by insomnia. Since last year, there have been an increasing number of reports saying children experience insomnia or sleep paralysis. Some of them came to the church for help. Others did not," Father William revealed.

I felt a gust of cold wind in the room suddenly.

"Insomnia used to be a normal thing. What makes this uncommon is that those who suffered from it had strange visions about a vintage book when they tried to sleep," Father William said.

"Is it the same book that I dreamt about?" I asked.

"I don't know. The strange thing is that, one by one, some of those victims were discovered later; they were never awake again...it is spreading like an epidemic." Father William uttered a sigh.

My mind went blank. I was stunned by those words.

Father William walked to his bookshelf. He climbed up the ladder and grabbed the third book from his right.

"I have been researching this for quite some time. I think I have some records about your dream as well as the vintage book." Father William descended the ladder and showed me his findings.

When he flipped through the pages, I could see Latin letters and strange pictures inside. One of the pages was showing a cave above a wide ledge. Another page was showing a vintage book with the symbol of a star inside a circle. Between the edges of the stars were strange looking characters, which didn't seem to be anything in English.

"Yes. It is exactly what I saw in my dream!" I exclaimed.

I flipped through a few more pages and saw pictures of historic invasions and wars.

The symbol appeared more frequently each page I turned.

When I looked at it more closely, I could see the image of the head of a goat.

"Father William, do you know what the symbol means?" I asked.

"This is a symbol to conjure demon. The symbol was written in ancient Hebrew writing. It says *Diary of the Underworld*," Father William said.

"*Diary of the Underworld*?" I was confused.

"It is a demonic diary that existed even before the bible. In ancient times, a group of higher archangels were cast out of heaven because of their desire to be God and rule all living things. These fallen angels rebelled against God and tried to prove God wrong that God did not know his children," Father William explained.

"Who are these fallen angels?"

"One of them frequently appears in the Bible. It deceives humans just like it deceived Eve to eat the forbidden fruit in the *Garden of Eden*."

"Do you mean Satan?"

"Yes. He has the aspect to bring evil and temptation to seduce humans into falsehood and sins. In the *Book of Revelation*, it recorded a War in Heaven. Satan and his legion of fallen archangels were defeated. The *Diary of the Underworld* records the dark sides of humanity. The fallen angels feed demonic energy from it. God, on the other hand, feeds on our prayers and faith. The *Diary of the Underworld* is supposed to be sealed by God, even from the angels. But, it seems that someone, or something, is trying to break the seal…"

"I wonder who would do such a thing?"

"I have no idea. But, right now, you must understand more about your dream. The book in your hand may guide you," Father William said.

"But, Father William, are you going to help me? I…I cannot do this alone." I sounded worry.

"Child, don't be afraid. We need your help now as much as you need ours. Only those who dreamed about the diary linger to it." Father William smiled at me and helped me to wear a silver cross. "Read this book and fall asleep. This silver cross will remind you this is only a dream. You will help us to locate the *Diary of the Underworld* through your dream. And we can seal it once again in the name of God. Only then will you be truly cleansed."

I uttered a long sigh. I really did not want to go back to that dream again.

I am just an ordinary girl.

Why did the *Diary of the Underworld* choose me?

Why do I have to go through this?

I really couldn't believe my insomnia is related to the *Diary of the Underworld*. But, I don't want to be the one who falls asleep one day and is never be able wake up again.

I looked at Father William and then this thick medieval book in my hand.

Will this book help me to understand my dream?

How can Father William locate this demonic diary though my dream?

Perhaps, reading is the only way to find out.

Slowly, I turned to the first chapter of the book and began to read.

PART 2

1462

9

Vlad was overlooking the paranormal view of Transylvania at the top of a watchtower.

The last sunrays of the day shone across the dreadful orange sky.

Hawks soared around the snow-covered mountain peaks.

The Ottoman Empire has passed like rain on the jagged mountains, like wind in the meadow. The army swiftly approached, shouting and rumbling. One by one, villages were burned to ashes. Peasants fled.

A woman called out to her children.

"Mina, Mina! Take your brother with you. You'll go faster with just the two of you." A mother put her little boy onto a horse in front of his sister.

"Mama! But Papa says Mina must not ride Odyssey. She is too big for him," Fred argued.

"Listen to me! The two of you must ride to Transylvania and raise an alarm. Do you understand me?" the mother ordered, eyes worried.

"Mama, we don't want to leave you! We want to stay

with you. We don't want to go." The children cried, tears slid down their cheeks.

The mother gave her children one big hug. Drops of water leaked from the corner of her eyes. Perhaps, this is the last chance she might be able to see her children ever again. But, for the survival of her children, she had no choice but to depart.

The eastern sky began to darken.

The orange sun hung low in the sky.

"Listen to me. I will find you there." The mother wiped away her tears and gave a watery smile.

Then they heard the roar and grunt of the Ottoman Empire closing in.

"Now go my children!" The mother gave Odyssey a pat on the back, shook the rein, and the horse started forward.

"Goodbye, my children." The mother looked at the back of her children as they disappeared into the shadow of the valleys.

***

On the banks of the Bran River, bodies of men and horses lie in the rain.

The once clear, smooth water stream is now dyed with red.

Below the watchtower, a scout scrambled his way up to where Vlad stood, gasping all the way.

"My Lord, Transylvania's defense is broken! We can't hold them! The city is ....is lost," Alexandros reported to his lord.

Vlad looked at Alexandros. He could sense a dreadful fear inside him.

"How many men do we have?" Vlad asked.

"One...one thousand," Alexandros stammered.

"And what about the Turks?" Vlad asked again.

"Ten...ten thousand?"

Vlad closed his eyes and uttered a long sigh.

The horrible death of his father and brother haunted him every moment. He could never forget how the boyars betrayed his father. The *Order of the Dragon*, he and his father serviced under the King of Hungary – an order to protect Eastern Europe and the Holy Roman Empire, was nothing but a lie. The boyars orchestrated wars between the Hungarian and the Ottoman Empire for their greed. And his father's throne was nothing but a puppet to the boyars.

Vlad vowed to avenge the death of his father.

The treachery of the boyars shall never be forgiven.

"We will retreat to Vambia, the last stronghold of Transylvania." Vlad gave a final order and descended the watchtower.

"My Lord, it will be a dangerous road to Vambia. We have to go through the mountains, and it will be slow. And we have women and children with us..." Alexandros doubted.

"Transylvania will not hold by next dawn. We must use the terrain to our advantage. That is why we must flee to Vambia. I will only do what I think is best for my people. We will march out tonight. Now, bring my horse," Vlad insisted.

Later in the day, Alexandros gathered everyone outside the Town hall.

He stood on a high wall, lifted his sword, and addressed a crowd of soldiers and peasants from below.

"By the order of the prince, the city must be empty. We make for the refuge of Vambia. Do not burden yourself with treasures. Bring only the provisions you need."

10

Mirena was wandering in the *Forever Garden*, encircled by the bed of purple flowers.

The fragrance of lavenders and the blossom flowers nearby brought her back the memories of her wedding.

Mirena could never forget her sensual moments with her husband.

She closed her eyes and tried to focus on that flash of memory she had with her lover in the lavender field. In her thoughts, she could not help but replay the conversation she had with him.

The whistling sound of the birds repeated in sweet melodious repeating notes.

She kneeled to pick flowers and put them in her flower basket. Her white sleeveless floor-length flower girl dress was absolutely stunning, making her a princess without equal.

It was dawn.

The sun hung low behind the jagged mountain.

Her husband should be back by now.

But, where is he?

The rattling sound of the birds chasing each other drew Mirena's attention.

She turned her head for a moment.

The purple roses waved at her under a gust of gentle wind.

There seemed to be a strange stillness over everything.

When she turned back to resume collecting flowers, a dark figure appeared in front of her that almost made her jump.

It was a man in dark leather armor. The man had rich chocolate curly hair. His eyes were a mesmerizing deep ocean blue. He had distinct cheekbones and an angular jaw. The handle of his sword was engraved with the symbol of the *Order of the Dragon*.

"I am sorry," the man whispered gently. "Did I scare you?"

Mirena looked at the warrior from top to bottom and then forced herself to look away.

"You flattered yourself," Mirena spoke and continued with what she was doing.

The man walked around and kneeled next to her.

"The purple roses. Are these for your husband?" Vlad asked. His eyes locked on the beautiful lady.

"They are ingredients for the feast tomorrow." Mirena raised her head and was held captive in the man's passionate glance.

Their gaze lasted for a full second.

"But is there a husband?" Vlad asked, pretending to look serious.

"Yes. And he maintains a natural interest in flowers," Mirena teased, she leaned herself closer to the handsome man.

"I am surprised. But he obviously has a keen appreciation of beauty," Vlad said playfully.

Mirena smiled, knowing too well Vlad was about to seduce her. Her resistance was about to crumble.

The warrior moved forward and brushed her long river of blonde hair.

Her breathing hastened.

Her heartbeat quickened and her lungs expanded.

The feeling had always been written in their gaze. It was chemistry, a seed of love since they met.

Slowly, gently, Vlad cupped his hands in Mirena's faces and sealed his kiss.

Both of them fell on the purple blanket of the garden.

Mirena pressed herself against Vlad's warm chest, not a word to be spoken.

Both knew that tomorrow would be a long day, a red day.

Suddenly, their romantic moment was interrupted by the sound of a cough.

It was Alexandros. He was standing at the entrance of the garden.

"Is it a bad time?" Alexandros asked.

"Perfectly fine to be truthful." Mirena raised to her feet and left the two men to discuss what is important.

"This better be important," Vlad rose from the garden and looked at his messenger.

"My Lord, I am afraid it is," Alexandros replied.

11

The red dawn surrendered to the darkness of the night.

Alexandros reported the enemy is advancing faster than they expected.

Prince Vlad ordered his troops to burn down his own village and poison the wells as they make for the refuge of Vambia.

"Let them come," Vlad gave the burning village one last gaze. Then he shook the rein and threw his horse to lead the way.

The night was long.

The stillness of the air was oppressive.

Vlad and his people marched through one forest after another.

An owl ruffled its feathers on an oak tree. Its yellow eyes were glowing in the darkness of the forest like a silent observer of the mountain.

At midnight, the wind roared like thunder and blew mercilessly.

Occasionally, they could hear the distant howling of

the wolves.

There was no sign of habitation.

After travelling for some distance, they arrived at the top of a summit.

Even in the evening mist, they vaguely caught a glimpse of a stone castle on top of a steep hill. Two summits behind the castle cut the sky, like a giant broken tooth. Below the castle were rivers like black ribbons that curled.

"What is this place?" Vlad motioned his finger to the barren castle.

"My Lord, this is Bran Castle. Vambia is just up ahead. In the meantime, we can use this castle as a defense against the Ottoman Empire," Alexandros suggested.

Vlad studied the terrain. The cliffside road was narrow and dangerous. The ledge was only a few meters wide without guardrails. His adrenaline soared as he looked down at the slope. Obviously, no horses were able to march from this point forward. Apparently, this trail was the only way up to the castle ahead.

Lightning cut zig-zag into the black sky.

Moments later came the rumbling thunder.

The horse began to neigh and snort and plunge widely. They reared as the soldiers in ropes tried to control them.

"Mama, I don't want to go to there," a boy cried as the brilliant flash of lightning illuminated the swooping bats circling the castle.

Peasants were exhausted after the long march. Some looked sad. Some held back their tears. Many were also reluctant to take the risk to cross the ledge in the dark-ness of the night.

"My lord, we must proceed with haste. The Turks are behind us. This storm might be a curse or a blessing. If we made it to Vambia, the village has supplies that can last us until the Turk retreats," Alexandros advised.

Vlad nodded and then addressed his unsettled army.

"Arise, my Romanian brothers. I see in your eyes the same fear that would take the heart of me! A night may come when the courage of men fails. But, it is not tonight. Tonight, we fight and defend our kingdom. Follow me to the fortress. Forth, and fear no darkness!"

12

Lucian led his Ottoman Empire into the abandoned city of Transylvania. Once they destroyed the *Order of the Dragon*, the conquest of Ottoman expansion would be unchallenged.

"General Lucian," a scout motioned to his discovery of the trail of footprints leading north.

Lucian dismounted from his horse and walked over to examine the size of the footprints. It seemed the Romanians had women and children among them.

"Don't worry, they won't be far." Lucian grinned.

When he looked back at his troops, it was long like a river.

His army has been pressing on for days. Never sleep. Never rest.

Everyone looked weary and exhausted.

"How long can our food supply last?" Lucian gestured a lieutenant responsible for army supply to come over.

"General Lucian, our food supply will be exhausted in fourteen days at most. The Legion won't be sustainable after that. Vlad III devastated every place he left behind.

There are no crops left behind," the lieutenant of the Ottoman Empire advised.

"Vlad III is cunning. Do not underestimate him. What about our logistic supply?" Lucian questioned.

"Recently, Naz and his left-wing party have been delaying our logistic supply. It will take another month before our next supply arrives," the lieutenant replied.

"Another month?" Lucian was surprised.

There was a long moment of silence.

No way it would take months for the logistic to arrive.

Naz has been gaming on his conquer and risking the lives of his troops.

He envied his countless victory in battles.

Lucian looked at his patriotic troops again. They risked their lives in battle.

It angered him to watch them purposely being starved to death because of some crazy politics.

Two more days…two more days is more than sufficient to conquer the remaining resistances of the Romanians.

The Ottoman Empire outnumbered their enemy.

It is only a matter of time before they can claim their victory.

"Let the soldiers rest," Lucian decided.

The Ottoman Empire encamped and began to rest inside the abandoned city.

***

Vlad and his troops had successfully arrived at the front gate of the Bran Castle.

It seemed the cliffside road could barely allow two soldiers to go through at a time.

Vlad had been observing the Ottoman Empire's every move since their invasion.

The enemy wanted a quick, short war because their logistic would take too long to replenish a troop of ten thousand men.

Without sufficient provisions to support a large army, the Turks could not persist long before they would reclaim Transylvania.

He returned his head and looked at this splendid castle in front of him – a fortress that can stand against the troop of ten thousand men.

The rain had finally stopped.

A dazzling sunlight broke out between the jagged mountain, and the sky went from pink to crimson.

"A red day. The sky is filled with the color of blood. Vambia will mark the grave of the Ottoman Empire. All we have to do is to drag the war as long as possible," Vlad vowed.

Later that day, Vlad assigned some of his scouts to look for Vambia and ordered Alexandros to settle the women and children inside the Bran Castle.

The interior of Bran Castle felt more like a royal piece of real estate. The dimly lit corridor and the thick velvet curtains made the place looked rather haunted. Inside every room are Gothic four-poster beds. When Vlad checked out the dining room, he saw it was decorated with statues and painting of boyars.

"My Lord, our archers are in position," a lieutenant reported as he led Vlad to the archery windows in the castle wall. They were facing the narrow cliffside road, which was perfect to shoot anyone who attempted to cross the ledge.

"Excellent defense," Vlad appraised.

Vlad arrived in a courtyard, while discussing his tactics with his advisors.

Soon, he saw a lady sitting next to a fountain in front of the balcony. Her beauty radiated like the sun among the crowd.

It was Mirena.

Vlad dismissed his advisors and walked towards his beautiful wife, smiling.

Mirena smiled, but had a roller coaster of emotions. Her gaze on him filled with love, worry, and sorrow. She was reluctant to see her husband go to war. The thought of losing him was suffocating.

Behind her, the Ottoman Empire encamped in Transylvania like a ribbon of river below, like a backdrop.

She wanted to leave this place with this man and start a new life with a different name, never to be heard of again.

"My Lady, you are so beautiful," a gentle smile spread across Vlad as a way to say good morning.

He placed a kiss at the corner of her mouth. His hand brushed several strands of hair from her cheek.

Mirena studied him and then took control of the kiss.

Vlad glanced at the threat below the balcony.

"Don't be afraid," he whispered softly in her ears and gave her a hug.

"My Lord, I will be with you wherever you go," Mirena pressed herself against his chest.

The heartbeat was strong.

All a sudden, her worries dissolved.

"I am sorry," Vlad wrapped his arm tightly around her back, holding her to his chest.

Mirena looked up at him. She knew her husband too well. He would always put his duty before his own feelings. It is part of what it takes to become the Order of the Dragon.

"Why would you be sorry," Mirena pretended.

"For not meeting you sooner," Vlad spoke as the Ottoman Empire began to march again.

Mirena knew her husband needed to depart.

"Will you love me until eternity?" Mirena asked, her eyes watery, but she closed her eyes and fought back tears.

"I will always, my love," Vlad gave her a soft smile. But, at the same time, it was full of sadness.

"The Turks are coming!" a guard in the watchtower above shouted and sounded the horn for battle.

"Come on people! Quickly, now!"

All a sudden, soldiers were hurrying to their positions.

Husband and sons were taken away from their mothers and wives to join the battle.

Weapons were handed out to the peasants.

They are frightened. Vlad can see it in their eyes.

"Mirena, mind the children, find food in Vambia when we return," Vlad said.

"My Lord, let me stand by your side." Mirena was reluctant to let him go.

Everything came so quickly, and she wasn't prepared.

"I am sorry," Vlad replied and ordered two soldiers to take Mirena away.

The sound of another horn drew their attention to the cliffside road below.

It was the enemy's horn.

The army of the Ottoman Empire slowly ascended from the mist, shouting and rumbling.

Once again, the crimson sky began to darken.

Streaks of lightning and rumble of thunder filled the sky, and it started to rain.

Lucian led his army forward, carrying torches, pikes, and spears.

Mirena and other women and children sat silently deep inside the dungeon of Bran castle, listening.

The Ottoman Empire pounded their weapons and roared.

Among them, a single rider appeared upon a dark horse.

The rider had full helmet and armor.

He shook his rein to move his horse forward to the edge of the ledge.

"Vlad III, Prince of Wallachia, please come forward," the dark rider shouted from the other side of the cliffside road.

Vlad stood high in the edge of the balcony of the castle. His velvet hood cloak was blown fiercely by the howling wind behind his blackish-red dragon armor.

"Welcome to my castle. I, Vlad III, bid you welcome," Vlad shouted.

Soldiers of the Ottoman Empire laughed at the humor of the Prince.

"Prince Vlad, I am afraid we do not come all the way to greet you and seek for peace. We come for your land.

Surrender now, disband your armies, and never return. Then I might spare your accursed life," the dark rider demanded.

Then an arrow accidentally fired from the archery windows in the castle wall and hit one of the enemy's man-at-arm in the helmet.

Everything went silent, as the man-at-arm felt, dead.

"I guess this concludes our negotiation," Vlad said as he disappeared from the sight of the enemy.

13

Lucian drew his sword and commanded his army to dismount their horses and cross the ledge.

"Archers ready! Show them no mercy! Their armor is weak at the neck. Fire!" Vlad commanded.

Bows were released from the Bran Castle, and the Ottoman Empire was showered with arrows. Many of the enemy soldiers fell down the bottomless ledge.

A group of men-at arm covered themselves in shields, trying to cross the cliffside road. But, the road was too slippery and narrow that almost made them slip.

"Let them try our catapults." Vlad directed his sword to the middle of the cliffside road and boulders were projected and blocked the pathway to the castle.

"General Lucian, the road to the castle is sealed. The rocks are wet. We cannot get through," one of the Ottoman Empire's lieutenant advised.

"Keep firing!" Vlad shouted and another round of arrows was shot.

"Damn!" Lucian stomped the floor in anger as his troop was suffering heavy casualties.

They tried to aim at the archeries in the Bran Castle, but the archery windows were far too narrow for their arrows to pierce through.

"Is this it? Is this all you can conjure?" Vlad insulted.

"Fall back! Fall back!" Lucian was forced to retreat.

There was no way they could reach this castle in this adverse terrain.

***

Vlad led his people back into the castle and celebrated their victory.

"The Turks have suffered a defeat today, but they will regroup. We must endure, exhaust their army supply, and then drive them out of our land," Vlad ordered.

Soldiers and peasants applauded and cheered Vlad's victory.

It was incredible that they just defended themselves against an army ten times their size.

But the victory was short lived when Alexandros came back with ill news.

"My Lord," Alexandros gasped as he hurried to the courtyard, where everyone was celebrating. He hesitated before he could speak another word. His eyes darted at Vlad, then to the crowds, and back to Vlad again.

The Prince read it in his eyes. Whatever news it is, it is best to be kept away from the crowd. So, he motioned Alexandros back inside the castle to have their secret conversation.

"Alexandros, have you managed to find Vambia?" Vlad asked.

"Yes. My Lord, I have found Vambia. But I have found

something more important," Alexandros gasped.

"What is it?" Vlad narrowed his eyes.

"There is a shortcut from Vambia leading straight back to Transylvania. The Turks will definitely look for other ways to reach Bran Castle; if they find this trail, we will -" Alexandros continued.

Vlad cut Alexandros off before he continued.

Alexandros is right.

The Turks will not give up looking for other ways.

Can they find a secret path hidden, even from the locals?

But, it is a risk they cannot take.

"Alexandros, take me to that trail. The Turks will definitely send scouts to look for other entrances after the defeat." Vlad grabbed his sword and followed.

The dusk drew near.

Vlad followed Alexandros and rode a curved mud path down to Vambia.

The trail curved under thick trees, and suddenly they were in the shade.

Even before the sunset, it was too dark to see anything. The leaves were so thick, and no sunlight filtered through.

They lashed their horses with long whips to march at full speed.

The hoofs thudded hard on the pavement, and the trees seemed to be hissing down at them.

Vlad thought it was a long, dark cobra slithering on the trees, but it turned out to be the sound of nature.

When the trees ended, they saw sunlight again.

The trail led them to a spot where they saw the same

summits that cut the sky like when they marched to Bran Castle yesterday evening.

Vlad and Alexandros pulled their rein as the horses began to strain and rear.

They dismounted to check the horses.

Alexandros petted and soothed them to quiet them down.

"The horses are frightened," Vlad puzzled.

"By what?" Alexandros looked around but found nothing unusual.

A curtain of flapping, chattering figures zoomed past them and flew all the way to the summits.

They shielded their eyes as the sun beamed down at them.

Even in the presence of daylight, they could see a swarm of bats was swirling around the summits.

"By bats," Vlad whispered.

Alexandros managed to calm the horses, and they continued with the way.

"Vambia is just up ahead," Alexandros said.

They turned another long, twisted road that led to a small town.

They dismounted the horses and walked along the cracking asphalt.

On their left were deserted farmhouses and meadows adjacent to one another. Lone peasants were busy harvesting crops.

On their right was a white church. Next to it was a cemetery with an unusually large number of tombs and cross.

When they looked up, they saw the shape of a broken tooth jagged between the summits, overlooking the whole town.

Everyone seemed expressionless as they walked by.

"Why is everyone like this? Don't they have manners?" Vlad asked.

Alexandros grabbed one of the villagers for questioning, but he tried to evade his grasp.

"No… not me, please. I want no part of this. I…I just want to live," the villager pleaded, shivering as he spoke.

"I am Prince Vlad III." Vlad grabbed the villager by the collar. "I want to know where is the village chief."

"Th…the village chief is in that church today," the villager stammered and pointed his finger to the white church.

"Thank you."

Vlad and Alexandros hurried across the cemetery. Several people dressed in black robes were moaning in front of tombstones.

This place is dreadful.

What is happening to this village?

As soon as they entered the church, they saw a clerk in a long white garment praying in front of a statue of Virgin Mary. Candles were flickering on the wall.

"I am the light of the world. If you follow me, you won't have to walk in darkness, because you will have the light that leads to life."

"For we are fighting flesh-and-blood enemies, evil rulers come for our land. Only by completely destroying our wicked enemy, my people will survive," Vlad interrupted.

The clerk turned around. Wrinkles spread across his face as he greeted the Prince and introduced himself as Noel - the village chief. He tried to kneel, but the Prince stopped him.

"There is a time to love and a time to hate, a time for war and a time for peace. In a world filled with sin, greed, and evil, war is inevitable," Vlad continued.

"Old man, did you or anyone in the village spot any unfamiliar faces lurking in the village since yesterday?" Alexandros questioned.

The village chief paused for a moment and shook his head.

Vlad and Alexandros uttered a long sigh of relief.

The Turks had not yet found out about the secret passage to Vambia.

"May I ask what is happening to the village?" Vlad asked as he gestured to the group of people moaning in the cemetery. In his mind, Vambia should be a remote, but beautiful village. But, it seemed that he was wrong.

"This village is accursed..." Noel sighed. "People are dying, not because of war, but something evil."

"I do not believe in evil spirits nonsense," Vlad rejected.

"But you must, my Prince." Noel insisted. "This is not a legend. It is happening. Vambia did not get its name by accident. High above the summits, behind Bran Castle, had a hideous monster trapped inside a cave. Few people sighted it. Few of those who sighted it would ever come back alive. Two months ago, an unknown disease has been spreading in the village. Crops are withering. Pastures are deserted. Those who get infected died smothering in their sleep. We suspect something evil is going on. It might be something to do with the cave."

"Alexandros, what do you think?" Vlad grinned.

"My Lord, this man has proven himself to be useful. This pitiful legend might be able to turn the tide of war in our favor." Alexandros smiled.

The old man continued to warn them, but Vlad and Alexandros walked out and continued to look for the secret trail from Transylvania.

Vlad walked past one of the tombstones.

In memory of Peter
son of Jack and Sarah Crutchfield,
who died April 22, 1462,
aged 13 and 21 days.

A middle-aged woman in black was moaning for her son who died just yesterday.

"How come I never heard of this legend before?" Vlad asked.

"My Lord, I am not surprised this ghost town is forgotten entirely. Vambia is a very small village. They pay so little in tax and not worth your time. I think the Black Death from a century ago weakened the Church. Now, even a cleric believes in a legend about demons and monsters," Alexandros answered.

"You are right indeed."

Later, Vlad ordered Alexandros to arrange supper and recruit peasants to defend the castle.

He went to check if he could find a way to seal the trail leading back to Transylvania.

Vlad followed the cracking asphalt road alone.

Long yellow grasses sprouting on both sides of the road were as tall as an adult.

The decaying dwellings on both sides had paint chipped in certain spots. The wood was worn down and scuffed up.

The wind was channeled to a low howl.

Soon, Vlad arrived in front of a large cave hole illuminated by natural light. This cave hole is so large the Ottoman Empire can easily march through it.

Vlad took a step forward as the cave opening towered over him like the mouth of an almighty worm.

This secret passage might be where peasants moved grains and crops to avoid consumption taxes imposed by the kingdom. No wonder Vambia has such a large piece of farmland, but they pay so little in tax.

This must be what Alexandros had been talking about, and I must find whatever it takes to seal it. Vlad decided.

Just as Vlad was about to turn back, he heard mutters from inside the cave.

Is it my imagination? Vlad squinted into the gray fog inside the cave.

Slowly, the mutters turned into whispers, and whispers turned into conversations.

He heard footsteps and saw a dim orange light glimmered in the abyss.

This is no good.

This must be the Turks.

They found the way to Vambia…

Vlad swiftly hid himself in the bush and camouflaged himself among the long yellow grasses.

Then he saw two figures in armor slowly appear from

the cave entrance.

They were scouts of the Ottoman Empire.

Vlad was thinking to draw his sword but then resisted the temptation to kill them. He was not sure if there were any more enemies behind.

The sky continued to darken. The place looked frightening.

The two scouts wandered aimlessly on the asphalt road.

"Sh – should we head back to the camp and tell the others we have found a village?" one of the scouts proposed.

"Of course not! Lucian sends us to find another way to the castle. He will kill us if this village led him to some other place. Besides, who will want to go back to the camp this quickly?" another scout argued.

"Bu –but, Lucian told us to go back as soon as we find the castle. We are running out of supplies," one guard proposed.

Vlad smiled when he heard the news. It is exactly what he predicted.

"Don't worry, we will find the castle. We will rest in the village tonight and head back tomorrow morning. Maybe they have some pretty ladies in the village."

The two scouts laughed and continued their way.

Vlad followed the two scouts from behind. He vowed they would not be going back to their camp alive, but he wanted to get more information about his enemy.

"That summit looks like the one Lucian has been talking about," one of the scouts pointed at the broken tooth shape jagged between the summits.

"Let's go there and have a glimpse, and we should head back down."

Vlad sheathed his long sword and kept a distance from the scouts.

The further they went up the hill, all signs of life vanished. Silvery moonlight made the hill shimmer. All the way up the steep slope, they saw scraggly trees poked up like skeletons. They travelled past one curtain of fog after another.

Occasionally, they spotted tilted gravestones on the side of the asphalt road.

Dozens of fluttering bats flew by and caused the trees to creak and rattle.

"Oh my god," one of the scout shrieked as a bat brushed against his helmet.

"Quiet, we don't know if there are any enemies around here," the other guard scolded.

"Why would anyone build a castle in such a hideous place?"

"How am I supposed to know? Let's get on with it."

An icy wind whistled on the hill. Leaves were whirling in a strong current before they settled on the dirt. Tall grasses were covered by frost and dew.

Finally, after a long struggle up the hill, they arrived at another cave.

"Where is the castle?" one of the scouts asked as he spun around.

"Huh? Where is it?" the other scout scratched his head.

They found themselves standing on a ledge. It made them faint just to gaze below.

"This castle must be on the other side of the cave," one of the scouts proposed.

The two scouts lit up their torches as they slowly began to enter the cave.

14

Vald followed the scouts to the entrance of the cave. He wanted to remain stealth, so maybe the cave would be a good spot to make them disappear forever.

Just when he decided to go in, a shrill scream from inside the cave made him shiver.

What is happening? Did someone attack the scouts before me? Who would that be?

Vlad lit a torch as he cautiously entered the cave.

His boot made a squish sound, and he almost slipped on the wet, damp cave floor.

Another bloody scream stunned him, and the cave went silent again.

Vlad followed the sound.

One by one, bloodshot eyes filled the cave.

Bats again. Hundreds and thousands of bats were hanging upside down in the cave.

Did the bats attack the scouts?

He looked around but didn't see any bodies.

"Young warrior, son of the dragon, I have been waiting for you," a ghostly whisper ahead drew his attention.

"Who is that?" Vlad spun around with his torch, and the bats were scared away.

Vlad followed the sound. He made a turn at the far end of the tunnel, and it widened into a deep, round chamber.

In the center of the chamber sat was a hideous winged humanoid creature with goat-horn and red scales. A purple tongue flapped from its jagged-tooth mouth. The creature stood at least nine feet tall. It had a muscular long tail with a sharp point that had one of the scouts impale high in the air.

Vlad looked at the creature in disgust as it suddenly wagged its tail and threw its prey onto the wall.

"I have been waiting for a man of your character for a long time, Prince Vlad III," the creature spoke in a hoarse voice.

"What are you?" Vlad replied and began to draw his sword.

"Neither enemy nor friend. In fact, I am just like you. I have been betrayed and sealed in this pitiful cave for 5000 years, never to see the day of lights." The creature walked in circle, condemned to this cave.

"Why are we the same?" Vlad questioned.

"Your father, Vlad Dracul, Vlad the Dragon, was murdered by your own noble boyars. Your brother, who was a prince before you, buried alive by the King of Hungary. Am I right? The boyars have been orchestrating wars between the Hungarian and the Ottoman Empire for decades. You are protecting a Kingdom that is merely treating you like a puppet in the name of a Prince," the creature explained.

"How do you know my past?" Vlad pointed the sword

at the creature.

"Oh. I know a lot about you. I can hear and sense through creatures in the wood," the creature snickered.

"What exactly are you?" Vlad studied the creature hard.

"Look at me. What do you see?" the creature hissed.

"I am looking at a monster," Vlad replied in disgust.

"Prince Vlad III, you are not looking at a monster; you are looking at your salvation." The creature uttered a wicked laugh that echoed through the cave.

"Salvation?" Vlad frowned.

"You should know by now, sooner or later, the Turks will figure out Vambia. What you are doing now is only delaying the inevitable," the creature explained.

The creature took out a vintage book from the center of the chamber. The book had the thickness of a bible. Its cover had the symbol of a star inside a circle. Between the edges of the stars were strange looking characters, which appeared to be Hebrew writing.

"I was once the highest-ranking Archangel in the Angrius Council," the creature spoke as it flipped through the pages.

"You really changed my impression of what an angel looks like," Vlad said sarcastically.

"Different Archangels have different aspects. I was the Archangel of Perfection, full of wisdom and perfect in beauty. I deserved to be worshipped like God, the Archangels of the Lord, in your Bible. I was the first Archangel, who was wise enough to advise the Angrius Council that humanity is a sin. I have been right. Greed and war blankets the Earth," the creature continued.

"How did the highest-ranking Archangel transform to become a monster?" Vlad questioned.

"There are neither absolute good or evil, my human friend. Some angels have the heart of a demon, while some demons can be genuine. Heaven and hell are just a step apart," the creature said as he flipped through another page. "Archangels from Heaven fed their immortality through human prayers. That is why they deceive you into worshipping them. The Archangels needs you as much as you need them."

"I…I know who you are now. You are Satan," Vlad stammered.

"Don't be afraid," Satan replied. "Endless years, I have watched you from the Underworld and saw your life filled with betrayals and vengeance. Your pain, your fear, and your desire for revenge made us stronger."

"How can you help me?" Vlad asked.

Satan stopped flipping suddenly. It seemed that he had found the right page in his book.

"Found it," Satan hissed.

"Why do you need a book?" Vlad asked.

"Diary of the Underworld is not a book. It is a Bible for demons. It recorded the sins of men and power of the dark. Not many mortals are worthy to inherit the power of the Underworld. You are just exceptional."

"What is the power of the dark?" Vlad pursued.

"It is a power that can help you to defeat the Ottoman Empire, seek revenge for your father, protect your wife and your people," Satan said as it held the *Diary of the Underworld* high in the air and began its ritual.

Slowly, the ground began to shake. The bats outside

began to flutter again.

A swirling black abyss appeared as a circle in front of him and then began to expand.

Then Vlad saw a crimson larva, the size of his hand, summoned from the abyss.

Satan grabbed the creature in one hand and killed it in his grasp.

"What are you doing?" Vlad was puzzled and shocked.

Satan didn't respond. He cut his forearm, cracked open a skull from the ground, and dripped his blood inside.

Vlad watched in disgust as he mixed the corpse of the dead crimson larva in his cup of blood.

"Drink." Satan offered. "Once you drink it, you will have the strength of ten thousand men. You will have superior self-healing ability. The forest will be your eyes and ears. Bats will be your ally. Your voice will bring terror and dread into the hearts of mortals. Your blood will be a scourge on this land."

Vlad looked at the bowl in silence.

In the reflection of Satan's blood, he saw a demonic version of himself. His eyes glittered like snakes. His face was pale.

"What will be the price if I drink this?" Vlad asked.

"Once you drink this, you will thirst for human blood. Once you feed, it will be like an addiction. Those bitten by you will become one of your kind. It will be like a plague. And at some point, you will lose complete control and murder your people and your wife. This is your curse," Satan explained.

"I will kill myself before I harm my wife," Vlad defended.

"We will see. For me, I will be set free after 5000 years. What do you think?" Satan said.

Vlad thought for a moment.

Sweet memories of Mirena and him filled his mind.

Is it worth to become a monster defending his kingdom? What does it mean for his relationship with Mirena? Will I scare Mirena away? Will I harm her?

Millions of questions filled his mind at once.

He put down the broken skull, just when he was about to drink.

"Give me a few days to decide," Vlad halted the offer as he exited the hideous cave.

15

*C*ock-a-doodle-doo

Morning had just arrived.

Roosters were crowing at the crimson sky.

Vlad slowly descended the broken tooth summit.

The mountains were silhouettes against the orange sky. The air felt refrigerated.

When Vlad shielded his eyes and looked further from the summit, he saw an ocean.

Maybe Satan is right. Not all demons are evil. Even somewhere as dreadful as Vambia also has a beautiful side.

Just as Vlad reached the bottom of the summit, he saw Alexandros waiting for him below.

"My Lord…" Alexandros gasped. His face looked worried.

"What is it?" Vlad gasped.

"It …it is Mirena. She -," Alexandros faltered.

Something isn't right.

"What happened to Mirena?" Vlad raise his voice.

"Mirena is dying. An enemy dart poisoned her. I was

travelling back and forth to find you, but you were no-where to be seen," Alexandros explained.

"How can she be harmed by an enemy dart while she is in the castle?" Vlad questioned.

"We …we are still investigating," Alexandros replied.

Without hesitation, Vlad followed Alexandros as they rode back to the castle.

But, how can an enemy harm Mirena with a poison dart, while she is protected in the castle?

"Hurry! Ja! Ja! Ja!" Vlad and Alexandros cracked their whips with wild cries of encouragement to urge their horses.

They travelled through the slopes of the wood and forest and eventually arrived at the Bran Castle.

Soldiers and peasants hurried to open the gate and greet their Prince.

Alexandros made way for the Prince to reach Mirena as he pushed through the crowd.

When Vlad arrived inside his room, he saw his beautiful wife in her white sleeveless floor-length flower girl dress. She was lying peacefully on the bed. Still. Unmoved.

Next to her were two doctors with their heads lowered.

Vlad's expression turned to sorrow.

"How…how is Mirena?" Vlad asked in pain, grabbing the doctors by the sleeves.

"My Lord, I am sorry," the doctors replied softly. "We have done everything we can."

Sorrow drove Vlad onto his knees. His lips trembled, and his shoulders heaved with emotions. His hands clenched into shaking fists.

A lone tear traced down his wobbling cheek.

Then another.

And another until heavy sobs streamed down his deep blue eyes.

Vlad reached out for his wife's hand. They felt cold and soft.

He could still smell the fragrance of lavender next to her.

But the once colorful world around him melted into grey.

Then he felt his wife's weak, gentle hand brush against his hair.

"It …it has been a magical trip to be with you this life. I … hate to break it to you, but I'm in a pretty bad shape now. I only have a few more hours to live. The sound of your tears is not the thing I like to carry with me to the grave. I would like to see your smile," Mirena whispered weakly.

"Why do you leave me now, sweetheart? Why so cruel?" Vlad grieved.

"Death is only in body, never in spirit. I'll always be around you – like the scent of purple roses that you and I breathe in the *Forever Garden*. Don't cry, my love. I will always be in your heart, loving you, looking out for you…"

One of the doctors showed Vlad the poison dart that murdered his wife.

"My Lord, our princess will ascend to Heaven among the angels. She will rest in peace. God will watch over her," the second doctor said.

"Silent! Mirena will not die!" Vlad roared as he stared at the poison dart for a long moment.

His sorrow slowly turned into wicked laughter when he heard the word God.

Peasants and soldiers' eyes opened in fear when they saw the Prince's drastic change. Peasants hovered over their children.

Dark clouds were looming over the horizon outside Bran castle. Cracks of lightning filled the sky.

"If God exists like you say, why doesn't it watch over Mirena, but take her away from me?" Vlad shouted. "God. Demons. Men are nothing but vessels to fuel their energy with prayers. What hope do men have in God when even the heart of demons shows me more generosity?"

Suddenly, Satan's words flashback in his mind.

Those bitten by you will become one of your kind.

Does that mean I will be able to save Mirena?

Vlad quickly pushed through the crowd and hurried back to his horse.

"My Lord, where are you going?" Alexandros's voice distanced from behind.

Vlad didn't have time to answer.

Sorrow and rage filled his mind.

Vlad vowed that whoever murdered Mirena would pay…

Right now, the most important thing was to save his wife.

16

"So, you finally made your decision," Satan spoke as Vlad re-entered the cave.

Vlad slowly walked into the chamber of the cave.

"I smell sorrow. I smell fear. I smell vengeance in your mind," the demon encircled the young Prince and sniffed. "What is troubling the young Prince?"

"Mirena is dead. Everyone I love leaves me one by one by betrayal and murder," Vlad sobbed. "I need the crimson blood. I need to possess the power to revive her."

"Very well. But, I have to warn you first. Once you drink, you will feel as if you were stabbed by thousands of knives before the transfusion is completed. Once you feed, it will be like an addiction. It will be irreversible."

"I will do whatever it takes. I am ready."

"Drink," Satan offered the dead crimson larva and his blood in the cracked skull once more. "Cast fear upon your enemy and those who betrayed you. You rage will fuel dark energy to break my seal. Your vengeance will add another page of dark glory in the *Diary of the Underworld.*"

Vlad held the broken skull and slowly began to drink. His lips were crimson with fresh blood, and the stream had trickled over his chin and stained his velvet hood cloak.

Vlad dropped the cracked skull onto the ground as soon as he emptied his drink.

All a sudden, his head felt tremendous pain like it was about to explode. His body shifted. Elongated fangs sprouted slowly from his blood dripping mouth. The front of his face, nose, and ears shape-shifted into the shape of a bat. His spine grew longer. He had developed a pair of demonic wings with talons, which could be deployed and retracted onto his back. His ears suddenly filled with sounds once impossible to hear. Swooping bats swirled around him like an aura of darkness.

Vlad screamed in pain during his transformation.

His scream echoed not only through the cave, but also across Vambia.

Slowly, everything became blurred.

Pieces of memories flashed in his mind.

Satan grimaced when he saw Vlad slowly being transformed into a vampire.

"Vlad III, the son of Dracul, is now the reborn as a devil of the Underworld," Satan spoke as his words slowly appeared in the *Diary of the Underworld*.

"His new name is Dracula."

17

Vlad felt like he was reborn as the transfusion was completed.

The image of Mirena flashed in Vlad's mind.

Vlad slowly got to his knees.

Then he shape-shifted back into his human form.

"You can read a person's memories when drinking their blood. No one can deceive you. Go now, son of devil; unleash your wrath to your enemy and those who betray you." Satan's voice filled his mind.

Vlad thanked Satan for the gift as he walked outside the chamber.

A colony of bats swiftly swirled around him again, protecting him.

Vlad increased his pace.

He dashed outside the cave and became part of the bat colony as he flew directly to the Bran castle at the speed of a falling star.

"Look! Dad," a child in Vambia pointed at the bat colony as it flew in the sky.

"The devil is here," his dad exclaimed as he collapsed

onto his knees.

Vlad landed onto the courtyard of Bran Castle right in front of a crowd. His aura of bats disbanded.

Soldiers and peasants' eyes opened in fear as they saw the superhuman strength of their Prince.

"Is…is that who I think he is?" one of the soldier stammered.

"No…he is not our Prince. He is a monster in disguise," A peasant screamed in fear.

"Papa. Mama." Children begin to cry when they heard the word monster.

Vlad was filled with rage as he sensed his people betraying him.

"Do not get in my way to save Mirena," Vlad spoke in a hoarse voice. He shape-shifted involuntarily as his pair of demonic wings deployed from his back.

"Monster!" peasants cried in fear as they fled.

Pikemen formed a formidable barrier with their wall of spear points.

A few men-at-arms were wielding their swords, standing by.

Suddenly, a huge net landed on him from above, which made his limbs and wings tangled.

Dozens of men were trying to pull the net and force Vlad on his knees.

Just when Vlad was immobilized, a few pikemen attempted to strike and impale their weapons right through the chest of Vlad.

Vlad spun backward and easily dodged the attack.

He tore the net apart using the talons from his elongated bat wings.

Two bolts ripped past his face and quavered onto a nearby stone pillar.

Vlad jumped backward onto the stone rail behind and stood straddling the crest of a ravine.

Everyone trembled as they saw the creature's supernatural speed. Their eyes filled with despair and fear.

Vlad descended from the pillar and shape-shifted back to his human form.

"Is this your loyalty? Is this your gratitude? Fools. You think you are all alive because you can fight?" Vlad scolded in a hoarse voice.

The soldiers lowered their heads.

"All of you are alive from the invasion of the Ottoman Empire because of me! It is because of what I did to save you!" Vlad roared.

"My Lord," Alexandros's voice came from a distance. "Mirena…she is…"

"Speak!" Vlad demanded.

"She just passed away…"

Without hesitation, Vlad rushed in the room where Mirena laid.

He saw his wife laying lifelessly on the bed. Both of her hands over her belly, holding a purple rose.

Vlad kneed down next to her and brush his hands gently against Mirena's forehead.

Rays of sunlight glimmered through the window, but he wouldn't see his shadow.

Not anymore.

"He is not our Prince!"

"He is a demon."

Vlad heard and felt the voices of mistrust from his

people through the sense of the swirling bats.

Slowly, he sank his fangs into Mirena's neck. But, her veins were not pulsing anymore.

He tried it again, but Mirena remained still.

The crimson blood does not work on those who are already dead.

But then, he read Mirena's memory.

He vaguely saw a boyar talking with a peasant in the doorway. They were secretly planning to strike a deal with the Ottoman Empire to overthrow the Prince. When they discovered Mirena eavesdropping, the boyar ordered the peasant to fire a poison dart at her neck.

When Vlad turned around, peasants gathered outside his room, holding torches. Among the crowd was a boyar in gold brocade or red patterned velvet. Broad sleeves extended to his wrists.

"Very well, grieve. I am Pyotr, the highest-ranking and noblest among all boyars. We have negotiated peace with the Turks, and you are endangering everyone's life just to have your vengeance for your father and brother. Demon. Today, we come to destroy you in the name of God," Pyotr said.

Then he ordered several pikemen to block Alexandros and prevent him from coming in to rescue the prince.

"Traitors," Vlad shrieked in rage, and he began to transform again.

Everyone was frightened of what their prince had become.

Screams filled the castle.

"Burn it! Burn the demon!" Pyotr yelled as peasants and soldiers incinerated the room with their torches.

It was too late for Vlad to run away.

"Nooooooo," Vlad shouted helplessly as the fire quickly spread across Mirena's bed.

Alexandros collapsed helplessly onto his knees.

The burning inferno engulfed everything in the room. Expensive royal furniture racked and wilted under the mercilessness of the orange flame.

Animal groans and moans filled with rage and hate.

The crowd trembled as they vaguely saw the figure of the humanoid creature dance back and forth in the sea of flame.

The intense blaze drove them backwards.

Black clouds of smoke choked the air above the Bran castle.

Then everything went silent.

18

A burning humanoid figure emerged from the flame.

Peasants and soldiers shivered when they saw the creature's wounds heal quickly.

The creature flexed its neck and uttered a high pitch, inhuman shriek.

"Pr...prince Vlad," one of the peasants stammered and dropped his weapon.

Despair filled the crowd as the hideous creature approached them step-by-step.

"Count Vladislaus Dragulia was born in 1422. Murdered in 1462. I am resurrected as Dracula, the son of devil," Dracula cried in a hoarse voice as he sank his fangs into the closest peasant.

The sky was crimson red.

Despair and dread filled the Bran castle.

Dying screams echoed across villages and mountains, so that even the Ottoman Empire from across the cliff-side road could hear it.

"Did you hear that?" one of the Turk soldiers asked.

"It seems like there is a bloodbath going on over the

other side of the mountain," another Turks soldier replied.

Lucian looked at his weak army. His army supply was depleted. There were insufficient provisions to last their trip home.

A guard collapsed onto the ground during patrol, exhausted.

The poison well left by Vlad had made the majority of his army very sick.

The intense heat under the sun and the landscape made it difficult for his army to assault.

And the two scouts he sent had not been heard of for days.

He overlooked the paranormal view of Transylvania at the top of a watchtower, but there were no signs of any logistic supply.

Lucian couldn't accept the fact that he was defeated.

He fought all the way to the town hall of Transylvania.

But, if he did not pull out in two days, he would be risking the lives of his entire army.

Perhaps, this is his destiny.

Just when he decided to call for a retreat, one of his lieutenants hurried towards him, gasping all the way.

"What is it?" Lucian asked suspiciously.

"General Lucian, you have to see this. We discovered a cave leading to a small village behind Bran castle," the lieutenant said.

"Do you mean the cave that our scouts left to explore?" Lucian questioned.

"Apparently, yes," his lieutenant replied.

"Where are the scouts? What have they been doing?

Do they know they have delayed and starved the entire army?" Lucian angered.

The lieutenant swallowed hard and didn't reply.

"I am asking you where are the two scouts?" Lucian repeated.

"Ge-general Lucian, the two scouts you sent died a horrible death. Their dried corpses were impaled right outside the village of Vambia."

19

Lucian gathered a few of his men through the dam cave to the village of Vambia.

His troops stared at the village in horror when they saw rows after rows of decaying corpses impaled by poles high above the ground.

There were women, children, as well as the enemies of the Turks among them.

A fat boyar in gold brocade and red patterned velvet had the end of a pole impaled through his rotting mouth.

Some peasants moaned in pain. Several peasants had slow, rattling gasps as they slowly passed away.

Vultures landed on the pillars to feed on the remains of the corpses.

The rotting smell of the dead made it impossible for Lucian and his troops to proceed.

Everything was silhouetted against the dreadful orange sky.

Lucian had been in war for so many years, but he had never seen this cruel scene.

Several soldiers vomited. Some soldiers fainted. Some

soldiers had gone mad and fled.

"Who would have done this?" one of the Turks soldier asked.

"Did another army invade them?" another Turks soldier suggested.

"This does not seem to be the work of any human." Lucian's eyes shielded away from the unbearable scene.

Lucian studied the wounds of the dried corpses.

Most of their wounds seemed to be inflicted by talons and claws rather than weapons.

And the strange thing is that most of corpses had bite marks on their necks.

"Did you see the bite marks?" Lucian motioned the evidence to his troops.

"Do…do you think they were attacked by some kind of animal?" the soldiers guessed.

"Which animal knows how to impale a human being?" other soldiers disagreed.

"Impalement is one of the most painful and cruel forms of execution. It is often used to punish traitors. If I am correct, these people must have betrayed the impaler," Lucian concluded.

He studied the ground, but there was no sign of any footprints.

It made him wonder who has the strength to impale thousands of men without leaving any traces of whom he truly is.

Everything was just too paranormal.

One of his scouts came back and reported the whole village was deserted. There was not a single survivor.

"We will claim this victory as our own. It is the Ottoman Empire that destroyed the last resistance of the Order of the Dragon. No one will say a word about what they see here today," Lucian ordered.

The Ottoman Empire left this mystery behind as Lucian led his Empire back home to claim his victory.

20

Satan walked out of the cave for the first time in five thousand years.

The sky was red – a color of anger, lust, and dread.

Satan gazed upon the magnificent scene of impalements in the village of Vambia.

So much hate. So much rage. So much fear.

Mirena's murder had turned Vlad into Dracula – a blood-thirsty vampire filled with love and hate.

The *Diary of the Underworld* glowed as it began to record the tragedy of what happened in Vambia today.

The sins of men have weakened Heaven.

Satan looked up in the sky.

It remembered its Archangel form as Lucifer – *the Light Bearer*.

It once had the highest of all positions among the angels. It had the highest attributes. Its position was to protect the holiness of God.

But then, it learnt that God's power came from the prayers of its children.

Once it learnt the secrets, it did not want to be the servant of the God of Angels. It desired to take over heaven. It wanted to be God.

I will ascend to heaven; I will raise my throne above the stars of God.

Together, with six other Archangels, they plotted to rebel against God and started the *Eternal Conflicts – the War in Heaven.*

However, they failed.

In its last moment of defeat, it still remembered how Archangel Michael, the highest of the heavenly angels, trampled it and threw it down to the Earth.

Satan flipped through the *Diary of the Underworld* and landed on a page. At the top of the page spelled the word *Lycanthrope.*

"I will need more power so that I can free my brothers from their imprisonment and rally the Legion of Hell. I shall have my revenge," Satan grimaced as he focused on the book. "Perhaps, you and *Dracula* will bring the game of rage and fear to the next level."

PART 3

21

Streaks of sunlight penetrated the window and blinded me.

I stretched my eyes above my head and yawned. My eyelids flickered and adjusted to the light in the room.

Then I saw Father William sat opposite me, smiling.

He was sipping his cup of *Espresso*.

"Oops. Did I wake you up?" Father William asked.

Wrinkles spread across his face.

"No." I said softly. I felt embarrassed for a moment.

How can I fall asleep in a church just like that? I punished myself.

Then I realized I fell asleep reading.

"Don't feel guilty, young lady. I fell asleep much longer than you the first time I read this book," Father William joked.

But, to be honest, this is the first time I felt so refreshed after sleep since I had insomnia.

Then pieces of my dream came back to my mind.

"Is the story about Satan true?" I asked.

"Satan escaped the cave where God sealed him," Father William nodded. "It knew that it cannot match the power of God. So, it waited. It deceives humanity and slowly skewed the power and balance between Heaven and Hell towards its favor. Until one day, when most people turn away from God. It will attack Heaven again with its brothers."

"What is the dream trying to tell me?" I asked.

"Alice, you are somehow related to the *Diary of the Underworld*. This is why you keep dreaming about it. Someone from the diary is desperate to meet you," Father William said.

"Will I get hurt?" I worried.

"Whoever is trying to find you, I don't think he is hostile to you. So, don't be afraid," Father William replied.

"How do you know?" I felt curious.

"Because I saw it in your dream while you were sleeping just then." Father William smiled as he retrieved the vintage book from my hand.

"I beg your pardon. You...you sneaked into my dream." I frowned.

Father William kept smiling but didn't reply. He tapped on my shoulder and led me to the entrance of the church.

When we arrived at the front gate of the St Mary cathedral, I saw Mom and Dad waiting for me. I thanked Father William once more for his hospitality and his silver cross.

Just as we were about to leave, I glanced at the clock on the ceiling to check the time.

Suddenly, I saw a dark shadow sweep by the stained-glass windows from the corner of my eyes.

Is someone watching me?

My eyes darted left and right in the empty cathedral.

But, everything was still and silent.

"Is there something wrong?" Father William asked as he followed my glance.

"Oh, it is nothing. Maybe it is just the wind," I replied.

22

It was a cool night.

I tossed and turned in bed as usual, trying to look for a comfortable position.

When I exhausted myself, I laid still in my soft bed.

I kept staring up at my ceiling.

Everything was dark.

I imagined myself staring at the entrance of a tunnel.

Scattered images of the tragedy of Vambia and the Bran castle flashed in my mind.

What type of pain did Dracula go through when the people he protected murdered his wife?

Can vengeance make him feel better?

Legends say vampires are immortal and ageless.

I wondered what he feels everyday waking up at night, missing the ones he loved, until eternity.

What kind of life does he live after losing everyone he loves?

Thoughts were circulating in my mind like a carousel.

Slowly, I began to close my eyes.

The carousel was coming to a stop.

I was drifting off to sleep.

***

Today is a normal school day.

I woke up early in the morning for school.

I slept incredible well last night.

Well, it might be because the silver cross Father William gave me really works on me. Who knows?

Renee messaged me last night that a new student is going to be transferred into our class. She was excited about it.

Mom dropped me off at the school entrance right before the school assembly.

Mrs. Berbhardt was standing in front of the gate, looking for any latecomers for detention. Renee and I once portrayed her as the Bulldog of Boston High. She is one of the most stubborn and fierce teachers we have ever met. But, the truth is, she is cold and distant on the outside, but warm and open inside.

RING!!

The school bell rang without mercy.

I gazed at my watch and it showed 8:29am.

I felt fortunate that I made it before the bell rang.

"Hey kid, what is your name? Which class are you in?" Mrs. Berbhardt barked behind me.

I turned around and saw an unfamiliar face.

The guy had the kind of face that can stop you in your tracks. He has prominent cheekbones and a well-defined chin. His skin was tanned. He has pale blue eyes and dark brown brows, which sloped downwards in a serious expression. I can hardly find any guy with those features in our school.

"I am new here," the guy finally spoke.

"I don't care whether you are new or not, you have broken the school rule. Now step aside on the other side," Mrs. Berbhardt scolded.

"Hey… Good morning, Mrs. Berbhardt," I drew the teacher's attention from behind. "You look very nice today!"

The clumsy teacher turned around.

"Alice, how are you? You aren't late today, are you?" Mrs. Berbhardt tilted her undersized Garamond light glasses as she looked at me.

"Umm…nope. I was just going to say thank you." I grimaced and hinted to the new guy to sneak in the school.

"Thank you for what?" Mrs. Berbhardt puzzled.

"Thank you for everything you taught me. You are such a great teacher. I hope I can have you as my teacher for next year." I tried to buy some more time.

"Oh. That is so sweet for you to say so." Mrs. Berbhardt said as she gave me a hug.

Now, I hope you know why I say Mrs. Berbhardt can be warm to students if you know the trick.

I quickly joined the assembly after I thanked Mrs. Berbhardt.

The assembly hall was big. Crowds of students of different nationalities gathered after a long weekend. Students were hustling and chattering. It felt like I was in a marketplace.

My eyes darted left and right, looking for Renee.

I wondered where she was because she usually arrives before me.

I spotted the new guy from my assembly line.

He seemed lost and wandered around when everyone was lining up.

"Hey, which class are you in?" I gestured him to come over.

"I should be in 7B," the guy spoke.

"I am in 7B too. Our line is just over there. My name is Alice," I introduced myself.

"I am Luke," Luke followed me. "Thank you for helping me out just then. Who is that fat lady guarding the school entrance, anyway?"

"Oh. You mean Mrs. Berbhardt. Everyone in school says she is one of the top teachers to avoid. But, the truth is that she is cold on the outside, but warm inside," I explained.

I couldn't take my eyes off him. He is kind of cute but weary. It is like he did not have enough sleep.

"Why did you transfer to Boston High?" I asked.

"I am new in town," Luke said.

"Attention everyone!" the sound of the microphone silenced the crowd.

Our principle led the morning assembly through prayers.

Strange. It was usually the head teachers who led the prayers. The principle will not lead the assembly unless something important is going to be announced.

Then there was a long moment of silence.

"It is with sadness that I inform you two of our students, Gina Wright, 7A, and Renee Hill, 7B, suffer sleep paralysis and slipped into coma last night. For those of you who know their name, we ask you to remember them. For those of you who did not know, we ask that you respect our sadness and support us with your understanding. It is very difficult for all of us to face departure of our young people. Students who need additional support should contact their school counselor. I would like you to join me in extending our heartfelt sympathy to their family," The principle announced, lowered his head and prayed.

The principle's speech sent chills down my spine.

Fear swept everyone like a plague. Everyone was discussing this shocking news. This was the second time students were reported suffering sudden coma after sleep paralysis and never woke up again.

Everyone thought it was an independent event.

Apparently, it is not. It is like an epidemic, and it is spreading.

Sorrow and sadness filled the assembly hall.

Then I recalled the words of Father William.

Those who suffered from insomnia had strange visions about a vintage book when they tried to sleep. One by one, some of those victims were discovered later; they were never to awake again...

No. This can't be happening.

Renee is my best friend. It cannot be Renee.

I broke out in tears and collapsed to my knees in despair.

23

I remained silent for the rest of the day.

I gazed at the empty spot where Renee used to sit.

Knowing that she might not be able to wake up again caused me pain.

Something evil is at work.

I need to see Father William again.

I held the silver cross tightly in my hand. My body shivered.

It was recess. A hand tapped my shoulder from the back and made me jump.

"Oops, I am sorry. I didn't mean to scare you," a voice spoke behind me.

It was Luke.

"I am sorry about your best friend, Renee," Luke spoke.

"No. It is not your fault," I replied.

I looked at him. His eyes were so narrow that he seemed drowsy.

"You looked exhausted." I raised my eyebrows.

"I know. But, you won't believe me. I am suffering

from insomnia," Luke said softly.

"Yo...you are suffering from insomnia?" I stammered.

Well, I am an expert on how that feels. It seems we have something in common.

"I have had insomnia for quite a long time. I couldn't get to sleep at night. Sometimes, whenever I take a nap, I have strange visions that repeat themselves," Luke explained.

Strange. It sounded exactly like me.

"What type of strange visions?" I questioned.

"I envisioned myself trapped in a dungeon of a medieval castle. Guards were patrolling above me. My neck was chained. I looked up at the silvery full moon. It was so pale, so beautiful. Its ambient energy showered over me. I wasn't alone. At the corner of the room were a few peasants. They were trembling in fear," Luke said softly.

"Maybe it is a movie you watched and the images keep repeating in your mind," I suggested. "I had a personal doctor, called Doctor Amy, who was treating my insomnia symptom. She told me that recurring dreams happen for many reasons. She told me that she once had a patient dream of being chased by a woolly mammoth somewhere in an African desert."

"That is pretty terrible," Luke said.

"It is. Dr. Amy said that patient is trying to get away from something in life or trying to hide from something he needs to face. It can also be a feeling the patient wants to avoid a conflict that he doesn't want to handle or a memory he would rather forget," I explained like Doctor Amy.

Luke paused a moment and then burst into laughter.

He looked quite charming with his pleasant smile.

"What is so funny?" I raised an eyebrow.

"It is nothing. I didn't have those dreams you talked about for a very long time," Luke explained himself.

"Oh. Okay. I hope you don't find me weird," I said.

The school bell rang. The recess was finally over.

The afternoon classes were math and science, which seemed to take forever.

School can be like a prison, especially when you sit for subjects that you love to hate. The teachers looked like as they were murmuring. Two girls in front of me were playing Tarot cards under their table. I gazed at the clock in the classroom occasionally, but was distracted by the empty seat of Renee.

Renee. Who did this to you?

Is it related to the evil of the *Diary of the Underworld* like Father William said?

I held the silver cross tightly in my hand.

I decided I have to tell Father William about this.

I really want to tell him.

I really do.

24

Life was ordinary for the next couple of days.

The silver cross did its magic on me. I slept soundly at night.

At home, Mom and Dad felt so glad that they do not need to worry about me anymore.

In school, Mary and Gina, who knew how to read Tarot cards, became really popular as pupils were asking them to make predictions.

"There is a young man in your life. He has rich chocolate curly hair. His eyes were mesmerizing deep ocean blue, and you are very important to each other," Mary glanced up at me with her chin still pointed down towards the cards.

The image of Vlad flashed in my mind. Interesting. But, how do they know?

"Yes," I said. "Yes, there is. What else can you read?"

My heart began beating faster in my chest.

"You love him, but you can't be together. But you should hold on and wait for him. He has been waiting for you for eternity. The separation isn't just about you. He loves you. He will find you when the time is right," Mary continued.

"Who is the lucky guy who has rich chocolate curly hair in class," one of the guy yelled.

Everyone looked around.

"Get real. Alice is the most beautiful girl in our grade. How would she pick monkeys in our class?" A chubby girl behind chimed in.

I felt embarrassed.

"Look, Alice's face is turning red," one of the guy teased.

"Thanks for the hints, Mary. I will have that hairstyle tomorrow," one of the guys joined.

Then I saw Luke leave the classroom at the corner of my eyes.

I don't understand why Luke seemed to have difficulties getting along with the class, both the guys and the girls. Apparently, he only talked openly to me.

Everyone will isolate him if he continues to behave the way he is.

I am a bit worried about him.

"Hey Alice, look at me. I have not finished yet," Mary snapped her finger to draw my attention.

"What is it?" I turned back to Mary.

Her expression changed suddenly.

There was a long moment of silence.

Next to her, Gina flipped the card over, and I saw a yellowed skeleton in black armor rode a pale white horse under a slate gray sky. Beneath him was a dead body laid out, a corpse whose crown had fallen from its head. A small baby and an adolescent girl knelt at the hooves of the marching horse, not fighting their fate. A bishop in ornate robes stands praying in the path of the horse. The sun is setting at the card's far right.

"What does that mean?" I asked curiously.

Mary and Gina exchanged glances with each other.

"Come on. Please tell me," I pursued.

"Come on. Please tell us," the rest of the class chimed in.

"This Tarot card represents death. It means death is involved in the first card you draw," Mary said.

"Death?" I began to feel nervous. "Can you tell me more?"

"Tarot card is divided into your past, your present, and your future. Death is probably best described in the past position. It shows you had a tragic past life. The warship off in the far distance means your past life was involved in some kind of war. The horse's leg is raised in a slow march on a certain path, meaning nothing will be spared."

Students were all excited. They were all interpreting the cards in their own way.

I looked at the card.

It reminds me of someone – Dracula.

"But –," Mary began to talk again, "even if it is a death card, there is some good news."

"What is the good news?" I asked.

"If you examine the card carefully, the sun is not completely set. This means that there are some opportunities, even though the coming change will be dreadful. When you look at the sky, you will see it is gray, not black." Mary explained.

"What is the difference between a gray sky and a black sky?" I asked.

"Black skies are the ones that give us no way out. But, the gray one is neutral. It means the coming changes you face might adversely affect you, and they might not," Mary predicted. "Last, when you looked at the skeleton rider, it is not looking directly at you. It is not a card that signals your death."

My eyes couldn't look away from the death card.

Statistics show that even the most inaccurate Tarot card reading is 75% accurate.

Is something bad going to happen to me?

Am I going to meet my true love?

Perhaps, only time can tell.

25

"Luke, wait up." I was trying to catch up with Luke after school, but he was too fast for me.

I kept shouting his name from behind, but he ignored me.

What is wrong with him?

When we approached at a pelican crossing ahead, a red light stopped him.

"Why do you ignore me?" I slumped over with my hands on my knees, gasping.

"Maybe you shouldn't be so involved into those… Tarot cards," Luke paused for a second and then said.

He was still looking away from me.

"Why are you so bossy?" I angered.

"I am not bossy. Tarot cards can sometimes attract evil," Lurk defended.

"No. They are just games. It is called trends. Everybody else plays it," I argued.

The green man signal flashed, and Luke continued his way.

We arrived at a street. On the opposite side of the street

116

are neighborhoods.

"Luke?" I tried to catch up with him again.

It was four in the afternoon. Dark clouds were looming in the sky. I felt a few drops of water on my forehead.

It seemed like it is about to rain.

"I just live a few blocks away. Do you need an umbrella?" I asked.

"No thanks," Luke said coldly.

"Did I upset you?" I felt sorry.

Suddenly, I heard a flap of wings.

Whoosh

Dogs in the neighborhoods flinched.

Birds scattered to the treetops.

Luke and I turned around and saw two dark figures descending from the sky. It was a male and a female, dressed in velvet lined, black dinner suit and dress.

Slowly, the two figures walked towards us and revealed their face. It was as pale as the full moon. Their skin was pallid and white. Their eyes were crimson red; their pupils were hyper dilated. Their eerie grin made us feel uneasy.

"Vampires," Luke whispered and motioned me to step behind him.

Did Luke just say vampires? How does Luke know? I rubbed my knuckles onto my eyes to make sure everything is real.

"Let's run. Aren't you afraid?" I pleaded.

"Oh, a Lycan and a human. Pitiful," the male vampire snickered.

Lycan? What is a Lycan?

"What do you want?" Luke barked at them.

"We don't want you. We want her. The vampire council is after the *Diary of the Underworld*. That girl is the key." The female vampire pointed her sharp nail at me.

What are they saying?

"I am sorry to disappoint you. I am afraid it is not going to be easy," Luke grinned.

The vampires hissed and snarled.

Step by step, Luke walked towards them. He flexed his neck. I could hear the shifting of bones. Fur sprouted and spread across his body.

I collapsed onto the ground in fear when I saw the front of Luke's face, nose, mouth, and chin grow into a short furry snout, and his canines and surrounding teeth naturally morphed longer into pointed fangs.

With a long, howl, it leapt for its attack.

26

I was running away aimlessly.

Everything passed by like flying color.

Everything seemed so unreal.

I can hardly believe I am friends with a monster.

The way Luke shape-shifted into a werewolf is just nightmarish. I thought vampires and werewolves only happened in Hollywood movies. I never know they can be real.

I turned my head after a while, but there was no sign of the beast nor the vampires.

So, I leaned my back against a tree to take a breath.

This can't be real. This can't be real. I told myself and held the silvery cross tightly with my shaking hands.

Can the Taro Cards be right? Is death near me? Why do the vampires say I am the key to the *Diary of the Underworld*?

Ouch!

I stumbled onto a broken log by accident and collapsed onto the ground.

A jagged stone cut in my right ankle. The wound was

deep. Blood oozed down like a river of red.

I tried to get back on my feet, but was halted when I spotted two vampiresses sniffing in the air, sniffing for me.

They were particularly easy to spot with their velvet lined, black dresses.

Slowly, I crouched silently and hid inside the closest shrub. I couldn't move a muscle.

"Where are you? I can smell you." The two vampiresses continued to sniff.

I squinted at the vampiresses from the gaps of the leaves.

Their grimace gave me goosebumps.

I could hear my heart pounding.

Sweat erupted from my forehead.

My stiff legs were injured and were no longer capable to escape.

27

Just as the vampiresses were about to reach out for me in the shrub, dark clouds were overtaken by streaks of orange and red.

Streak of orange sunlight showered on the two vampiresses without mercy.

The two immortals tried to shield their melting face with their hands as they uttered a high pitch scream. Their velvet lined, black dresses began to incinerate as the sunlight intensified.

Before I could react, a hand covered my mouth and pulled me out of the shrub.

It was Luke.

He returned to his human form. Wounded.

I just realized he was injured trying to protect me.

I was frightened by his wolf form, but touched by his valor.

The two of us stared at the dying vampiresses as they slowly crumbled into ashes.

"Don't be afraid. I mean no harm," Luke spoke softly, covering his wound with one hand to stop the bleeding.

"Yo...you are hurt." I worried. "I need to take you to hospital. I will ask Mom to drive you to Kensington Medical Center. It is not far from here."

"Hospital?" Luke laughed. "Don't worry about me. The moonlight will heal me. Right now, I am more worried about you. The night is no longer safe. They have found you,"

"Who are they?" I asked.

"They are vampires seeking the *Diary of the Underworld*," Luke explained.

"Why are the vampires after this accursed book?" I asked.

"The vampires believe the *Diary of the Underworld* possesses a dark ritual that can give them the ability to walk in daylight, much like Dracula," Luke said, glancing at the ashes of the vampiresses. "The Lycans and the vampires have been fighting a war that lasted for centuries. Our war has driven both species to the brink of extinction."

"Why would Lycans and vampires fight each other?" I asked.

"It is a long story," Luke said as he began to explain.

PART 4

28

Two centuries had passed since the tragedy of Vambia, and Transylvania became an abandoned place.

Those armies that attempted to invade Bran Castle never returned.

Rumors soon spread throughout Romania that Vlad III is a blood-thirsty monster. He would sit in the battlefield at mealtime and drink blood from his dying victims.

Soon, Vlad the Impaler, the demonized Prince of Romania, became renowned as Dracula.

To safeguard himself against both the Hungarians and the Turks, Dracula had created his Legion of undead.

Over the years, his armies grew.

But, even as immortals, Dracula realized his descendants were vulnerable to sunlight.

It is their curse.

His army of undead couldn't travel far to invade other nations. So, they were forced to remain inside the fortress of Bran Castle.

Even as an Elder Vampire, Dracula was not unchallenged.

His borders were constantly troubled by the growing threat of humanity during the day. They sought vengeance for what Dracula did.

At last, countries joined forces for the first time in history to eradicate their common enemy – Dracula.

This grave news drew the attention of the vampire cavern.

"Count, the Turks and the Hungarians have allied to invade our fortress. The Turks will attack us from the East and the Hungarians will attack us from the West. There are more than twenty thousand soldiers. They will be here in three days," A vampire scout reported.

"Three days?" the council members looked at one another in shock.

A wave of worries swept over the vampire cavern suddenly.

"Silence," Dracula roared.

At last, Dracula's nightmare had come true. He anticipated the humans would unite and storm the Bran Castle one day in their most vulnerable state - while the vampires slept.

"We will guard the Bran Castle during the day," Dracula spoke.

The whole vampire cavern looked at him in disbelief.

"Count, this is suicide. How can we guard the Bran Castle while we cannot even be exposed to the light of day?" one of the council members asked.

"The sun will burn us into ashes before the enemy strikes," another council member joined.

Dracula paused for a moment.

The council members may be right.

Unlike him, the vampire cavern is weak.

Time was running short. There were few options left to sail through their risk of extinction. They can either eradicate the human army during the night, or they need something dangerous to guard the Bran castle during the day.

Right now, both choices are nothing more than wishful thinking.

After an unproductive meeting, Dracula spent the night at the courtyard alone, like he always did.

He had been doing this everyday for the past two centuries.

Every time he is here alone, he remembers his beloved wife, Mirena.

He remembered seeing her sitting next to a fountain in front of the balcony. And her beauty radiated like that of the sun among the crowds.

That was the last time he saw her.

He promised her to love her until eternity.

And he still does.

Ironically, he lived an eternal life, but she was no longer here…

Then the sense of the bats in the wood interrupted his thoughts.

They were like their eyes and ears.

He could feel the enemies were approaching, day and night.

His enemies were well-prepared.

The catapults and ballista they brought were enough to tear down the Bran castle.

"Count, we followed your order and captured that beast in the wood. It is being held captive by our guards at the very bottom of the dungeon," a vampire warrior reported.

Dracula smiled. This beast can possibly change the tide of war towards their favor.

"Show it to me," Dracula ordered as he followed the vampire warrior.

They travelled down a spiral stairway in a stone tower. The atmosphere was dark and suspenseful. The medieval stonewalls felt cold and damp. Sometimes, they could hear the sound of the rhythmical ocean waves.

After a few twists and turns, they finally arrived at the dungeon – a place where they kept human prisoners.

The prisoners tried to reach out for the Count behind the iron bars when they walked by. But, the vampire guards drove them back with the cracking of whips.

Moans filled the entire place with dread, just as the Count would have wanted.

Betrayal by his people that led the death of his wife made him the ruthless Dracula he is today.

People often say time can heal everything, but centuries had passed since the murder of his wife; he could never forgive, never forget.

29

Dracula arrived at the entrance of an isolated part of the dungeon.

The beast he ordered his guards to capture was in the chamber up ahead.

Even at a distance, the dungeon was filled with the sound of animal breathing and growling.

The vampire warrior walked the Count inside the chamber.

Then they saw it.

The beast stood about eight feet tall, chained to the floor. It was covered with gray hair. It had a dog-like face, featuring ivory-white fangs, pointed ears, and glittering golden eyes. It flared its nostrils, as it smelt the presence of Dracula. Then it curled up its gums to reveal its yellow stained teeth.

Four vampire guards cracked their whips on it, trying to tame it by force.

"Such a magnificent beast," Dracula grimaced and walked towards the creature.

"Count, beware. This wolf took out several of our

men before we captured it," the vampire warrior warned.

"This is no natural wolf. It is a Lycan," Dracula spoke.

"A Lycan?" the vampire warrior puzzled.

"Like vampirism, lycanthropes are curses recorded in the *Diary of the Underworld*. Unlike werewolves, which can only transform under a full moon, lycans can transform into a wolf form at any time of the day, at any place. They are immune to silver and are much smarter, fiercer creatures." Dracula explained as he took another step towards the lycan.

The lycan sniffed and grunted. It turned its ominous golden gaze on the vampire.

"Count, we found these gears next to the beast," the vampire warrior said as he handed over an old sword used by commander of the Ottoman Empire long time ago.

The Count examined this antique sword carefully.

Apparently, this sword seemed to be at least two hundred years old. The hilt of the sword was engraved with the word Lucian.

Lucian. Such a familiar name.

"Count, why did you ask us to capture this accursed beast? Shouldn't we be preparing for the war against the humans instead?" the vampire warrior asked.

"No. We are already preparing for the war," Dracula spoke softly. "Bring them in."

Two vampire guards held the prisoners' leashes and collars and forced them into the lycan chamber.

The prisoners were paralyzed with fear when they saw the hideous beast. They tried to scream, but no sound came out.

The vampire guards cracked their whips onto the prisoners and forced them close to the lycan.

Moonlight showered through a barred window into the lycan chamber.

The lycan locked on its prey; its jaw unhinged into a grin. Its teeth gnashed frenziedly.

With a howl, it lowered its head and began to feed.

30

The corpses of the prisoners lay still on the stone floor.

Their dying screams sent shivers and chills to the rest of the dungeon.

The vampire warriors watched with joy and blood lust as the chamber soon became a river of red.

Dracula studied the creature with his eyes, his face grim.

Intrinsically, every cell in his body told him to slay the lycan. But, he ignored them.

An aura of gloom and despair engulfed his mind like a poisonous fog.

"Take the bodies away," the vampire warriors ordered the remaining startled prisoners from a distance.

Then the vampires began to leave.

"Count, are you planning to use this wild beast alone to fight against the human empire?" one of the vampire warrior asked.

"This beast is the only hope we have got." Dracula gave him a sneered grin.

The vampires frowned, puzzled by their master.

What ability did a lycan possess to help the vampires change the tide of the war?

But, it didn't take them long to find out their master's intention.

A shrill scream from behind them drew the vampires' attention.

Just as they turned around, they watched in horror as the corpses of the prisoners began to reanimate and transfigure under the moonlight. Their bones broke. Their human skin shredded. Paws tore their way through their hands. Their heads elongated and their body covered with fur. Their teeth were replaced by a set of canine teeth.

With a loud howl, they attacked the prisoners who were supposed to pick up their body.

"Run!" a prisoner tried to escape, but the fangs sank into his neck.

One vampire warrior tried to stop the lycans but was knocked out almost instantly by their giant paws. Another vampire tried to jam a dagger into a lycan's back but gave up as soon as the lycan turned around and flared its monstrous fangs. The monster struck with its tail and knocked the vampire from his feet, smacked hard onto the stone wall.

Drat!

A crossbow bolt darted towards a lycan, and it uttered a pain-filled hiss.

Dracula ordered the vampire bowmen to fire a handful of arrows and drove the lycans back.

Then they quickly locked the iron gate.

The rest of the vampires grasped their swords tensely.

They were surprised by the strength of the newborn lycans.

"This lycan will be a key to our war." Dracula smiled. "They will guard the Bran castle during the day. They will exhaust the humans, and we will attack them at night."

"Should we make more?" the vampire warrior suggested.

"We will," Dracula smiled and exited the dungeon.

31

"So, did the lycans help the vampires to defend the Brad Castle?" I pursued.

"We did," Luke gazed skyward.

It was night time already. The sky was clear and starless. Moonlight showered over us in the lavender garden.

I lost track of time listening to Luke's story.

"It was a victory orchestrated by the vampires. Killing my own people isn't something I enjoy, even though I am no longer a human," Luke continued.

"Are...are you the great general that led the Ottoman Empire to invade Romania in the fifteenth century?" I guessed.

"That is correct," Luke nodded. "I was Lucian the Great."

"But...but, you were victorious in the Ottoman expansion. What happened to you afterwards?" I was confused.

"I wouldn't call it victorious, even though it is how history is written. The truth is that we never conquered

Vambia. That was the work of demons. Soon after I returned to Turk, I was condemned by the King. Naz and his left-wing party blended the truth and accused me of sparing Prince Vlad's life because we never found his corpse. To prove them wrong, one day, I decided to travel to Vambia to investigate what actually happened, then I met him," Lucian said.

"Who did you meet?" I asked.

"I met a mysterious man hooded in a dark cloak." Lucian continued. "He told me what I saw in Vambia was the work of a devil called Dracula. He said he would offer me the power of *lycanthropy* in exchange for destroying Dracula. I gladly accepted until the *lycanthropy* took over me. I murdered innocents for the lust of their flesh. I became a monster. Everyone was hunting me. So, I decided to hide myself in the wood, away from people. Slowly, I had forgotten my identity. I had forgotten my wife and children. I had forgotten my mission," Luke uttered a long sigh.

I felt sorry for Lucian. He must be very lonely.

"But, you were helping the vampires in the past. What makes you turn against them now?" I questioned.

Lucian turned around and continued his story.

***

"For Count Dracula," the vampire council celebrated with the blood of their enemies after their glorious victory.

Dracula watched the outrageous lycans multiply in numbers. They slaughtered both the Hungarians and the Turks and eventually drove them outside the Count's border.

Even the threat of the humans was over. Dracula sensed a new threat that was growing by the day – the lycans.

So, one day, Dracula gathered everyone and told them what to do with the lycans in the name of celebrating for their victory.

"My Council, the lycans helped the vampires to score a remarkable victory and secured the border of the Bran castle. The human threat is now no more. Cheers!" Dracula cheered and emptied a glass of his enemies' blood.

The council gestured their glass in response and celebrated.

"Count, we should allow some of the lycans into the castle and join our rank," one of the council members suggested.

"No, lycans are slaves. They will always be slaves," another council member disagreed.

"But the lycans helped us to defeat the human empire."

The council became divided, just as Dracula expected.

"Silence," Dracula cut them off, and everyone listened.

"The lycans defended us from the human invasion. They saved us from our extinction. And we have all seen that," Dracula spoke.

The vampire cavern all agreed.

"But, they can potentially be a new threat if we do not take them out now," Dracula continued to explain. "Their number grew. Their power has grown. They are physically more powerful and can attack us during the day when we are vulnerable."

The vampire cavern began to alert.

"But, their numbers are not the deadliest," Dracula said.

"Count, if it is not their number, what else is the deadliest?" the vampire cavern asked.

Dracula asked his guards to bring an antique sword forward and show it to the council members.

"It is a common enemy you are all familiar with from a long time ago. It is Lucian, the general of the Ottoman Empire from two centuries ago," Dracula revealed.

"It is impossible. I still remember how Lucian's army brought destruction to every village he conquered," an old vampire said, its eyes wide with fear.

"Count, you may be right. But, Lucian helped us. He is no longer our enemy," a council member disagreed.

"Lucian helped us because he has been a lycan for so long. Everything he did for us was driven by his animal spirit. But, if Lucian realizes his past one day, he will attack us. We do not risk things getting out of control," Dracula speculated.

"Count, what do you suggest we do?" the vampire cavern asked.

"We must imprison Lucian deep under the dungeon of the Bran Castle for now. We slaughter the rest of the lycans and make sure the power always stays in the hands of the vampires."

32

The day after Dracula's speech, Lucian was imprisoned.

Lycans were puzzled as their master was locked away from them all a sudden.

Their numbers were greatly reduced when the vampires fed them with poisons.

Before the lycans realized what happened, it was already too late.

Some of the remaining lycans were captured. Others fled into the woods.

Lucian, on the other hand, slowly regained his human memories after the war against the humans. He couldn't handle the fact that most of the Ottoman Empire died by his own hands. He watched helplessly as his lycan brothers fell into the evil plan of Dracula.

The mysterious man hooded in dark cloak lied to him.

Lycanthropy is not a gift. It is a curse.

Now, he is locked away from others, deep in the abyss of an accursed dungeon.

The vampires betrayed him. They used him, and he played right into their hands.

Lucian punished himself. He vowed to destroy the vampire cavern. But, right now, he is too weak. He must wait for the right moment to assassinate his worst enemy - Dracula.

***

Several years later, on a full moon day, most vampires had lowered their guards against Lucian.

New and young vampire guards guarding his chamber replaced old faces. Whenever he asked them about Lucian, most of them thought he was only fiction. Almost all of them believed it were the vampires who won the war against the human invasion.

When the moonlight showered over his chamber again, he managed to escape.

That night, Dracula was in his courtyard alone, battling against the oppressive monotony of his eternal life.

Behind him, Lucian was approaching one step at a time.

"Lucian, what does betrayal taste like?" Dracula asked with his back facing his old enemy.

"Not as sweet as my vengeance, you devil!" Lucian howled as it transformed into a lycan under the moonlight.

"Unfortunately, hell has no vacancies." Dracula smiled as he turned around to face the lycan.

"You knew I was coming?" Lucian was puzzled.

"I can't tell you how happy I am that I can meet a pure lycan. I knew this moment would come. Maybe you can give me death. My name is Dracula, lucky in battle and nothing else. Put me out of my misery." Dracula sneered. His eyes gleamed with contempt.

Lucian leapt up and growled. He raised its paw and began to attack.

Dracula deployed his pair of demonic wings. With a screech, he shot up high above the courtyard.

Lucian spun around and looked up in the dark sky, but his enemy was lost from sight.

A cold whoosh of air passed, leaving a deep and jagged cut on the lycan's back.

The lycan howled in pain as another whoosh of air scratched its face.

Dracula decided to land on the ledge of the castle, watching the lycan snarl and wave its paws aimlessly at the air.

Soon, the lycan exhausted itself and collapsed onto the ground.

"Come and fight me, you bat!" Lucian roared with rage.

Before Lucian realized, dozens of vampire guards surrounded him.

Something was wrong. He was ambushed.

The vampire guards were wearing chain mail from head to toe. Some guards hummed their longsword in their hand, blade glimmering with a radiant light. Some guards charged their way with their heavy broadsword. Others had crossbow pointed at the lycan.

"Kill the lycan! Kill the lycan!"

The vampires chanted.

The crowd was in a frenzy.

Lucian dodged naturally as a vampire guard tried to

jam a dagger in his back. It seized its prey and delivered a lethal blow.

A vampire warrior slashed broadsword at the lycan but missed it by an inch. The lycan lifted him up and threw him off the courtyard, down the mountain.

Two other vampires bellowed and charged.

CLANG!

They swung their sword but banged the tip of their blade on the stonewall.

Lucian rolled and scrambled away.

He saw Dracula on the rooftop and tried to climb the castle wall.

ZIP!

Two bolts ripped past, missed Lucian's face, and quavered onto the stonewall.

ZIP!

Lucian screamed in pain as an arrow imbedded in his ankle!

ZIP! ZIP! ZIP!

Two more arrows embedded themselves onto the lycan's back when its claws grasped the ledge where Dracula stood.

Lucian was fainting. The blurry image of Dracula towered over him under the full moon.

It uttered one final battle cry before it lost its grasp.

33

Deep in the woods of Transylvania, the lycans that escaped the massacre of the vampires were alerted by a howl.

It was a battle cry from their master.

Soon, the forest began to rumble.

Thousands upon thousands of werewolves and lycans swarmed towards the Bran castle like a plague.

The subtle changes in the forest drew Dracula's attention.

"Count," a vampire warrior began to ask but was silenced by his master.

Lucian could felt his troops from the earth-shaking ground.

The lycan packs leapt over the boulders, pounding and scraping as they left a sandstorm behind them. They plunged madly towards the castle with extraordinary speed.

Before the vampires realized what happened, the wolf packs emerged from the mist and fog outside the castle.

The roar of the wolves sounded nearer and nearer, as

if they were closing in from every side.

Dracula quickly ordered his vampire troops to gear up and guard the gate. Vampire archers went in position of the battlements.

ZIP! ZIP! ZIP!

Arrows rained down from the castle, and dozens of lycans collapsed on the ground.

The lycan packs ignored the arrows and kept advancing.

The noble council member watched in fear as lycans and werewolves climbed the castle wall swiftly. They roared with anger and sent the bowmen straight down the castle with a swipe of their paws.

The lycan attack caught Dracula by surprise.

The Count thrust his sword, and his vampire warriors drew their blades in preparation for combats.

Blood spilled in the night.

Dracula and Lucian watched the spectacular fight of the two races.

They stared at each other with rage, ignoring the fear-filled screams and howls of fury.

This fight had been delayed for two centuries.

"You are not running away this time, Dracula." Lucian roared with rage as his eyes locked on the Count.

The lycans outnumbered the vampires, but the Count didn't seem worried.

He disappeared under a manhole the moment Lucia looked away.

Lucian transformed back to his human form and followed the vampire down the manhole.

The first orange hued rays of sunrise appeared between the broken tooth summits. The sunlight defined the victory of the werewolves as the sunlight set the vampires on fire instantly.

Lycans and werewolves uttered a victorious howl when the vampire cavern in the Bran Castle was no more.

34

"Dracula, show yourself. It is over," Lucian yelled in the abyss as he cautiously walked in an unknown part of the Bran Castle.

His voice echoed down the hollow sewage.

It was like a labyrinth down there.

He could hear nothing but the constant sound of dripping water.

Lucian ventured aimlessly.

It was quiet. Too quiet.

Whoosh!

Lucian ducked just in time as a sword whistled over his head.

He rolled behind a pillar, twirling his blade in the air.

"Impressive." Dracula appeared like a phantom in the abyss, his face pale and cold.

"I have been waiting for this for two centuries," Lucian spoke and drove his sword into the heart of the undead.

Parry.

Clang!

"You and me, we have been at war before either of

us even existed." Dracula wielded his blade to exit the parry.

Lucian cried out in agony, and they changed positions.

"What do you mean?" Lucian asked breathlessly.

"Our immortality came from the *Diary of the Underworld* – a book that records the sin of men. Do you really know why Satan created us?" Dracula asked.

"I do not know who Satan is. All I know is that I am created to destroy you." Lucian roared as he stabbed the vampire in the chest.

Lucian was surprised when Dracula didn't dodge.

The blade went right through Dracula's heart!

Dracula cried in pain. His eyes opened wide in fear. Bleeding from the wound.

Just as Lucian thought he had killed the ancient vampire, Dracula's expression changed. The horrific look on his face turned into a grin.

"I am Dracula, born in 1422, murdered in 1462. I am revived as an immortal, because I made a deal with Satan. My rage and vengeance towards humanity will fuel Satan's power," Dracula said. "Do you think Satan granted you the power to destroy me? He grants you power because he wants to feed on your rage towards the vampire. From today onwards, the vampires and lycans will have eternal conflict. All our sins will be recorded in the *Diary of the Underworld*."

35

Lucian felt lost.

He watched Dracula disappear inside the abyss.

For two centuries, he thought *Lycanthropy* could grant him the power to kill the vampire.

But, it failed him.

Lycanthropy and *vampirism* are nothing more than curses to fuel rage.

They are tools used by Satan to feed on the ugly side of humanity.

Perhaps, Dracula is right.

Maybe a greater evil is orchestrating hate between the two races.

Lucian climbed back up from the sewer.

It is a new day.

Bright streaks of pink and orange overcame the darkness of the twilight sky.

The vampire cavern that haunted this place for centuries is no more.

Lucian was pleased when he watched his lycan brothers worked together to rebuild the Bran Castle.

They saved his life.

Although the vampires suffered a big defeat tonight, it wasn't over.

As long as the *Diary of the Underworld* exists, evil will prevail.

PART 5

36

I was astonished to hear Lucian had such an incredible history with Dracula. I never knew both species, both summoned from the *Diary of the Underworld*, had so much hate with one another.

"In the past five centuries, the lycans and vampires battled each other to the brink of extinction. I lost many brothers along the way. Our rage and hate had finally fed Satan enough power. The sins recorded in the *Diary of the Underworld* helped Satan to open a portal so that he and his Legion can attack Heaven. When that happens, the rage of the angels and demon will make this place a living hell. That is why I must destroy the *Diary of the Underworld*," Lucian said.

"But, what about the vampires? Do they have the same agenda?" I asked.

"Unlikely, the vampires are blinded by the dark power within the *Diary of the Underworld*." Lucian doubted.

"How long do we have before Satan opens that portal?" I questioned.

"The day is close. I can feel it with my psionic power.

That is why it attracts many creatures of the Underworld here. The Bible once mentioned that, when the sun turn to darkness and the moon to blood, the great and dreadful day of the Lord comes," Lucian quoted.

"A red moon? That will be tomorrow night during the lunar eclipse," I speculated.

"There is not much time," Lucian spoke.

"But, how do we know how to find Satan?" I was puzzled.

"The same method you call to God. But in a different church." Lucian explained.

"Which is?" I was confused.

"The church of Satan," Lucian replied.

That night, Lucian safeguarded me home.

He soothed the cut in my right ankle under the moonlight, and it healed almost instantly.

I gazed at the gentle side of the beast when it had its hands over my wound. But, when he lifted his head and looked at me, I dropped my gaze.

I felt its love and gentleness.

I wasn't afraid of it anymore.

"Do you still feel the pain?" Lucian asked. His pupils turned yellow without his notice.

"A little," I replied softly. "But I live just a few blocks away. I guess I will be -."

Lucian lifted me on his back before I could finish.

My scream soon turned into laughter. Everything happened so quickly.

"You weigh like a feather," Lucian joked.

"Do I?" My face turned red. I felt embarrassed.

My heart was pounding so fast, like it was going to

jump out of my chest.

Slowly, I formed a bond with the lycan.

We talked and joked with each other on the way home on the quiet street under the moon.

The fur of its back felt so warm, so smooth.

I felt so comfortable resting on his back. Slowly, I drifted into sleep.

37

When I opened my eyes again, I was lying comfortably on my bed.

It was Saturday. That meant there was no school today.

My windows were opened and a message was left on my desk.

Cute.

It was from Lucian. He asked me to meet him at the St Mary Cathedral at noon.

Why St Mary Cathedral? Isn't it a Holy place?

Well, maybe I just need to go there and find out.

I had breakfast with my parents, and they wondered why I stayed in my room all night.

I told them I had go and thank Father William again for treating my insomnia, and they gladly agreed.

It was a cloudy Saturday. The clouds that had been wispy white in the morning now became darker and dense. The gloom of the day was reflected in the mood of the people.

I stood for a while to wait for the bus to St Mary

Cathedral. The queue was long. The bus was unusually crowded. I almost stood for the whole trip until two people got off, and I slid into a seat.

The bus bounced along the street. I stared out at the passing houses and yards. Howling wind blew fiercely on the street. Rain paddled against the windscreen. A baby started crying in the back.

Why do I have a bad feeling about today? I always trusted my intuition. Something is going to happen today.

I kept thinking about what happened yesterday.

Everything seemed so unreal. But, I saw them with my own eyes.

When I glanced out at the window again, I realized I had definitely passed my stop. I saw trees and strange looking buildings I'd never seen before.

I pressed the button and the bus squealed to a stop. I squeezed past the crowd through the aisle and hurried outside the back door.

A truck rumbled past, sending out puffs of black exhaust behind it. I waited for it to go by and hurried across the street. There was no one else on the sidewalk.

I hurried all the way back to the St Mary Cathedral, gasping.

Dark clouds hung low over the roof of the church. It seemed like a heavy rainstorm is on its way.

I peered through the stained-glass window.

But, it seemed empty.

I would have expected Father William would have a mass.

Oh well, maybe not at this time of the day.

I checked my watch, and it was almost one.

Slowly, I entered the church. Flock of pigeons flapped violently as they exited through the door. My sneakers thundered loudly as I walked inside the church. Streaks of lightning illuminated images and patterns of the stained-glass windows.

One of the images showed an archangel vanquishing Satan and crushing it under his feet.

I walked on the carpet between the rows of wooden church chairs.

"Father William?" I called.

No reply.

"Lucian?"

No reply.

A loud, rumbling thunder cracked the stillness of the air, as if it tried to crack the heavens apart.

I ducked involuntarily with each thunderous boom.

The harmony was a lot different from last Sunday.

I cried the names again.

No reply.

Another flash of lightning illuminated the statues of angels as if they were staring at me.

Don't be afraid.

A hollow voice echoed in the church.

"I recognize you." I recalled the voice in my dream. I recalled the voice that night outside my house.

As I spun around, I saw a mysterious man hooded in a dark cloak appear behind a pillar.

But, it disappeared and reappeared like a phantom when I approached him.

"Why are you appearing in my recurring dream?" I

asked.

"You are so different from others. You looked like her. So special. So pure. So elegant," the phantom said.

I was confused.

"Excuse me. But, who are you?" I felt something wasn't right.

"Mirena. Don't you remember me anymore?" the phantom said softly.

Mirena?

The images of Vlad III and his wife in the Forever Garden flashed in my mind.

"Is…is that Vlad?" I guessed.

The phantom sang.

Look at love
How it tangles
With the one fall in love

Look at spirit
How it fuses with earth
Giving it new life

How does he know this song? I remembered only Vlad heard me sing that before.

"Do you know life's most beautiful things are not seen with the eyes, but felt with your heart?" the phantom spoke gently.

I remembered Vlad had told me this before.

Just as I began to race towards the phantom, I hesitated. I remembered the horrible things he did in Vambia and to the lycans.

"Why did you do horrible things," I asked.

"Forgive me, I did what I had to survive. I have been so lonely for all these years. I tried to avenge you. But revenge did not make me feel any better. An eye for an eye makes us all blind. Relieve me, Mirena. You have the purest blood. I need a drop of your blood to end this vampirism curse. Forgive me, my love." The phantom lowered his head.

I felt sympathy towards Vlad. The loss of his wife made him a demon. Betrayal and rage corrupted his soul.

Even as a devil, he never forgot his wife.

I will release him. I told myself. I will release him with my blood.

My minded seemed clouded.

Step by step, I stumbled my way towards the phantom.

I heard a whoosh and I began seeing red on my wrist.

"I have been waiting for this moment all these years." The phantom slowly unhooded and revealed himself. "However, I am not your beloved Dracula."

38

The hideous humanoid creature had goat-horn and red scales. A purple tongue flapped from its jagged-tooth mouth. It shredded its cloak with the spread of its wings. The creature stood at least nine feet tall. Its left hand was holding a vintage book. Its right hand was armed with a trident. Its long muscular tail wagged left and right and a wooden church chair splintered.

"Yo...you are Satan?" I stammered. I was too frightened to resist.

"That is correct," Satan said in a hoarse voice.

"Why do you choose me?" I asked weakly.

"You are Mirena reincarnated. Your death was the real reason Vlad became Dracula. It is the reason his love for you turns into wrath." Satan laughed.

"Did you plan all this?" I continued to ask.

"Of course. I was the one who awakened the devil inside Dracula. I was the one who orchestrated the war between the lycans and the vampires. Greed and war fed me power. When the blood moon hung low tonight, with one drop of your virgin blood, I will be able to open the portal of the Underworld to invade Heaven, once again. I will be God. This is the final chapter of the *Diary of the Underworld.*" Satan uttered a horrible laugh.

My body felt weak. I felt my soul slowly drifting away from my body.

"Now. You will soon join your friend, Renee," Satan began to cast a spell and rip my soul away.

39

I found myself lying on a symbol of a star inside a circle, my body curled like a fetus.

On the edge of the stars were five candles.

The giant red moon hung low in the sky.

The whole place was blanketed by a dreadful red mist.

I studied my surroundings and realized I wasn't alone.

I saw Renee, Gina, and other kids that had gone missing, because of insomnia, all laid in a similar symbol.

Satan was murmuring spells on a stage under the red moon, conjuring demons from the *Diary of the Underworld*.

Father William was held to a cross below the stage like Jesus.

Suddenly, the once magnificent St Mary Cathedral became the church of Satan.

Black abyss of the Underworld swirled and expanded on the ground like black holes. The voices of pain and despair channeled through them.

A giant talon suddenly exposed from the black hole made me scream at the top of my lungs. The creature uttered sibilant hissing as it climbed out of the abyss. I opened my eyes in horror as the blind creature had an exposed brain tissue with a total loss of skin. Its elongated tongue looked like a whip as it moved. Then, it scrabbled out of view, trailing sticky fluids in its path.

More and more creatures scrambled out of the abyss as Satan continued to conjure them.

Suddenly, a loud roar came from nowhere that made everyone turn around.

It was Lucian and Dracula.

"I thought the two of you should would be fighting each other over Alice," Satan mocked.

"You deceived us into helping you," Lucian cried angrily.

"I thought you would never figure it out. The two of you are merely disposable puppets of my grand plan." Satan laughed. "Vampires and Lycans are merely C grade creatures in the underworld. There is very little difference between you and the hell spawns climbing out of the abyss right now. But, once my ritual is complete, the gap of the abyss will be wide enough for higher grade creatures to squeeze through."

Lucian flexed its neck and transformed himself into its lycan form. It uttered a battle cry and charged at Satan with full speed.

Dracula shape-sifted. Swooping bats swirled around him like an aura. It deployed its pair of demonic wings with talons and joined Lucian in the attack.

Satan was forced to halt the ritual. And the portal from the underworld began to close.

"Wretched creatures, you decided to join forces against me? Have you forgotten I am your creator?"

Satan grimaced.

The three creatures battled fiercely on the stage. Blood dripped from their injuries, lathered with sweat.

Parry.

Clang!

I climbed to my feet and stumbled my way to the priest. I used my numbed finger to untie the knots for Father William.

"Father William, are you okay?" I asked weakly.

Father William collapsed onto the ground, sweating.

"I am sorry, Alice. I am really sorry." Father William looked regretful, gasping as he spoke.

"Sorry? What are you sorry about?" I was puzzled by his sudden apology.

40

"One year ago, I was very sick. Satan paid me a visit and offered me immortality so that I can cheat death and ease my suffering of my long-term illness. In return, I must help him to look for Mirena reincarnated and gather one hundred virgin souls by the next lunar eclipse – the next red moon rise. He granted me the necromancy ability with his *Diary of the Underworld* so I can search through people's dream, create fear through nightmares, and steal their souls," Father William explained.

"So, you knew everything from the beginning! Yes. My insomnia symptom happened exactly one year ago. You tricked me into believing you!" I was astonished, and backed away.

"I am reborn as a dream demon," Father William said as he began to change. "I have no choice but to gather the souls of your friends and others. Only then can Satan relieve me from suffering."

I grabbed my silver cross that I wore but finally realized the cross was inverted.

It is an anti-Christian symbol.

Father William's eyes closed. His face began to deflate and flowed slowly inside his body. His body was swollen, rippling with strange muscles. His right arm was at least five inches longer that his left.

At the same time, sorrowful faces were forming, growing, rising from his chest. They were the people that had been kidnapped in their dreams! I saw Dr. Amy. Renee and Gina…

Their souls were all swallowed…

At last, a red, nightmarish mouth with razor sharp teeth cracked open in his stomach, uttering a furious cry.

Oh my god.

"Father William, please…" I collapse to the ground. My feet were numb. I jerked back with my trembling hands.

"That is right. I am the dream demon," Father William snarled, his voice changed. "I have possessed inside him for a long, long time.

"No. You are not. You are Father William, a Christian loved by many people. You christened me when I was a little. You are not a monster!" I protested, but my voice came out weakly.

"Do you know why you are not yet one of them?" the creature asked as it pointed its talons to the deflated faces on its body.

I shook my shivering head.

"I realized you are Mirena the moment you dream read the vintage book. I could have devoured you in your dream. But, you had such a deep connection with

Dracula, the man who loved you for his eternal life. Your blood means a lot to Master Satan. But now, the ritual is almost over. You will soon join your friends," the creature continued.

I was too shaky to respond.

I watched helplessly as the shadow of the dream demon slowly casted over me.

The creature raised its mighty talons and began to attack.

41

*D*racula - ?

My eyes opened when the talons torn right through a velvet hood cloak. Crimson red blood was streaming down the shredded part of the hood.

"Dracula, you die trying to protect this human. Why?" the dream demon asked.

"Be…because she is the only… reason I live," the vampire said weakly.

The dream demon released its talons, and the vampire collapsed onto the ground.

Lucian raised his head and uttered a long sorrowful howl under the red moon.

Puffs of dark cloud gathered and surrounded the moon from all sides.

Oh no, the ritual –

Satan screamed in rage. Gas billowed from both of his goat horns.

Creatures of the Underworld quickly crawled back into the swirling abyss as they began to contract and disappear.

"Dracula, why so silly? Why?" I rushed towards the dying vampire and held him by my arms, sobbing as I spoke.

Dracula slowly changed back into his human form.

He rolled to my side and looked at me with his pale eyes. His features were soft like when we first met. His heart thumped in rhythm with his slow, shallow breath.

"It is good to be able to see you again," the vampire smiled.

"No... don't speak. Just rest. I am with you. I will always be with you." I felt emotions swirl over me. I clutched his cold hands.

I felt the muscles of my chin tremble.

Then a pearl-shape tear ran down my cheek onto the vampire's face.

Then another.

And another before it came pouring down like rain.

Dracula's hand moved slowly behind his velvet hood. Then I saw a purple rose.

"You kept that?" My shoulders heaved with emotions.

"Death is only in body and never in spirit. I'd always be around you – like the scent of purple roses that you and I breathe in the *Forever Garden*. Don't cry, my love. I will always be in your heart, loving you, looking out for you..."

Cock-a-doodle-doo.

Morning had just arrived.

Roosters were crowing at the crimson sky.

"Good-bye, my dear," Dracula slowly faded into particles as the sunlight shone.

"No. No. No. There are still a lot of moments I want to

spend with you! There are still a lot of moments I want to spend with you!" I scrambled myself to shield him from the sunlight with his velvet hood cloak.

Lucian tried to block the sunlight, but it intensified every second.

At the end, all that remained on the ground was a purple rose.

42

"Satan, do you know sacrifice is the highest of all love. Dracula sacrificed himself to save and protect the woman he loved. He had written the final chapter in the *Diary of the Underworld*. The world will continue to fill with love like it always does. The power of hate and fear is no more. You, with your abomination, will be banished back to the Underworld where you belong." A voice came down through the cracks from the clouds.

"I will ascend to heaven; I will raise my throne above the stars of God." Satan roared in rage as he charged towards the sky with his trident.

But it stopped as soon as the blinding sunbeam shone on him.

Crushing pain throbbed violently around his skull, forcing him to collapse from the sky.

Suddenly, a lightning bolt like the fist of Heaven came crushing down and banished Satan and his abomination back to the Underworld.

Lucian smiled when God lifted his lycanthrope curse.

The evil plan of Satan is no more.

I didn't tell others about my experience. I doubt anyone would believe me either.

Later that week, the school principle made an announcement that Gina Wright and Renee Hill had finally recovered.

Children that were declared in a coma by doctors mysteriously awakened one after another.

The doctors said they couldn't explain their sudden recovery. They joked that it was the work of God.

The truth is that it really is.

For the first time since last year, I can finally get some rest.

"Alice, it is time to go to church," Mom shouted from downstairs.

"Just a second," I yelled back as usual.

I was sitting in front of my makeup table, being indecisive which color to put on again.

Crimson? Purple? Pink?

What do you think?

I gazed at the purple rose on my desk.

But, the scent was no longer there.

Purple rose is a symbol of enchantment. They are long-lasting.

I closed my eyes, letting my mind fill with our moments.

I never knew we had such a beautiful and sorrowful history when I first met him in the lavender garden that day. I didn't understand why he had a sad smile.

I wondered what this legendary monster felt everyday for the past five centuries, missing his beloved wife.

He must have felt lonely.

I finally understand what he means by long-lasting.

True love is timeless…it is eternal…

I remembered the look of his deep blue ocean eyes when he first met me in the garden.

I cried involuntarily again.

He had never forgotten about his wife…

After church that day, Mom drove past the garden where I first met Vlad.

I asked Mom to drop me off nearby so that I could spend some time with the flowers.

I sat silently on a boulder on a small cliff.

A gust of wind made a column of lavender flowers swirl up in front of me.

Everything felt so silent. So peaceful.

I spend the rest of the day enjoying the stunning purple sky above the lavender field.

Life's most beautiful things are not seen with the eyes, but felt with the heart.

Vlad is right.

I can feel him.

He will always live inside my memory and my heart.

Until eternity.

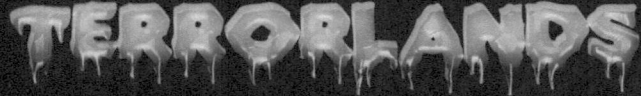

TERRORLANDS

Reader Beaware : You May be in for a scare

MARCO CHU KWAN CHING

 https://www.facebook.com/terrorlands/    https://twitter.com/terrorlands

About the Author

Marco Chu Kwan Ching's books are read all over the world. Apart from the Terrorlands Series, Marco Chu Kwan Ching is also the author of two books, *Corruption of Real Money* and *Legacy of Debt*.

You can learn more about his work at

www.terrorlands.com

www.corruptionofrealmoney.com

When he is not writing, he loves working on Fiverr. He has thousands of happy customers around the world.

https://www.fiverr.com/mckcvision

Marco Chu Kwan Ching lives in Australia with his wife, Carrie.

Thank you for Reading!

If you love my work, please feel free to leave a positive feedback on Amazon and Goodreads.

My contact:
https://www.facebook.com/marco.chu.10
https://www.goodreads.com/author/show/15944678.Marco_Chu_Kwan_Ching

Terrorlands Facebook Page
https://www.facebook.com/terrorlands/

Terrorlands Twitter Page
https://twitter.com/terrorlands

Goodreads Page
https://www.goodreads.com/book/show/34313163-diary-of-the-underworld

Terrorlands Website
http://www.terrorlands.com